CAPTAIN SATAN:
THE AMBASSADOR FROM HELL

THE AMBASSADOR
FROM HELL

By William O'Sullivan

ALTUS PRESS • 2019

CHAPTER 1
THE TRIGGER OF THE LAW

CARY ADAIR moved his rangy frame in a deck chair on his penthouse terrace, high above the financial canyons of downtown New York. His keen gray eyes rested for a moment on the rugged, square features of Jo Desher, dynamic Chief of the Federal Bureau of Investigation—the most talented group of crime smashers in the United States.

Desher, long a confidant of the apparently care-free and undoubtedly wealthy Cary Adair, was twirling a tall glass in his strong hand, his eyes on the iced, amber fluid.

"Sure you won't change your mind and have a highball, instead of plain ginger ale?" Adair asked.

The crack investigator of the F.B.I. shook his head. "Thanks, no." He looked at his wrist watch. "It's nearly two P.M. now, Cary. My car ought to be along any moment, to take me to Brayton, up in Westchester County."

Adair's almost severely clean-cut features were eased by a faint smile. He knew his friend well enough to reason that the purpose behind his visit was to "think out loud" about some case he was working on. In the nine years that Desher had known Adair, there had sprung up between them a sort of Sherlock Holmes-Doctor Watson relationship.

Jo Desher, the "Holmes" of the pair, had more than once profited by the incisiveness, the sharpness, of Adair's mind...

a mind singularly acute in its perceptions of criminal psychology for a man who was obviously a clubman-idler—a reserved, suave man-about-town.

And Cary Adair, owner of the skyscraper office building atop which he made a luxurious and secluded, if strange, home, took

Satan fired rapidly through
the bedlam of noise and blood
and his bullets struck home.

a deep interest in the other-than-routine cases which Jo Desher recounted to him from time to time.

Adair was too canny to prod his F.B.I. friend, was quick to sense those moments when Desher would speak of some problem that he was turning over in his mind. But he knew the signs... knew Desher's refusal of a drink to be a sure sign, now, as they sat on the sun-drenched terrace that looked down over New York Bay, that he would soon speak.

Adair looked around at a sound from the wall-wide studio window of his apartment. His manservant, Jeremy Watkyns, was almost noiselessly removing the dishes from the table where Desher and Adair had partaken of a light, cold lunch. Tall, gaunt, clad in somber black, the man moved with deceptive speed, his dark, brooding eyes and lean face grave, his slender, long-fingered hands transferring china and silver from table to tray with magic deftness.

Adair stifled his impatience in the continued silence, eased his powerfully muscled body while he sought and found his expensive cigarette case. He selected a smoke, fired it with a barrel-shaped enamel-and-gold automatic lighter. The movement seemed to stir Desher.

"Funny affair, up at Brayton," he said suddenly. "I'm going to take a look at it. The New York field office made a check of the— er—alleged *facts*." He stressed the last word, seemed to place it on the still air and consider it. Adair smiled openly, showing strong, white teeth against his healthily browned skin.

"What do you mean by 'alleged facts,' Jo?" His voice was that of a well-schooled pupil asking the proper question.

Desher surged his compact body forward in his chair, his brown eyes meeting Adair's squarely. "The Bank of Brayton, within the last forty-eight hours, has discovered a shortage of seventy-five thousand dollars, Cary."

"Is that an *alleged* fact?"

"No. That's a known fact. But it doesn't concern us—doesn't come into the realm of the F.B.I."

"Why not?"

"It isn't a National bank, Cary; and it has no Government funds on deposit." He paused, rubbed his chin reflectively. "Six months ago it had some W.P.A. funds in its charge. But they were paid out for local project work. So it's out of our hands."

Adair nodded. "So it's just another case of embezzlement, eh? Where do you come into it, then?"

"The F.B.I. enters the case through the *alleged* facts, Cary. It seems that in the course of the State investigation, an extortion note for just that sum of money—seventy-five thousand dollars—turned up among the effects of the bank's president, one Calvin Cossart."

"Oh, oh!" Adair's eyes notched up their interest. "Cossart *borrowed* the money, eh? Does he claim he paid it to the extortioner... to the threatener?"

JO DESHER shook his head slowly. He patted his breast pocket, frowned. "Now, what the devil did I do with my cigars?" he muttered.

Adair's manservant glided soundlessly onto the terrace, a Panama hat in his hand. He deftly produced a half-dozen wickedly black cigars and proffered them to the F.B.I. man. "In your hat, sir," he murmured.

The F.B.I. investigator riveted the gaunt man with a bleak stare. "I'm on to your sleight-of-hand tricks, Jeremy," he said severely. "But, when you 'lift' my cigars, you might absently return me some of your boss's sixty-five cent wonders, instead of these ropes!"

Adair grinned. "You cost me money that time, Jeremy. Give Mr. Desher a box of my specials."

Desher lighted up, blew a cloud of fragrant bluish smoke, and returned to his subject again. "No, Cary, Calvin Cossart doesn't claim he took the money to pay his threatener. As a matter of *alleged* fact, he claims that he knows nothing of the missing money… he claims that he never before saw the threatening note that was found in his safety deposit box—*with* a negligible amount of the vanished bills. The numbers check, by the way. And he claims that while he had access to the vaults, he hadn't been in them for more than a month. Says he had no cause to be near them."

Adair frowned. "What do you mean, Jo? You sound as if you had proof that it was he who took the money?"

Desher nodded. "We have. Some of the vanished bills were in his deposit box. His fingerprints turned up on *new* securities in the vault… although he claims he hasn't been in the big safe in a month. And he was in the bank, alone, the night before the money disappeared. Finally, we found his fingerprints on the threatening letter… the letter he claims he never saw."

"Pretty conclusive," Desher shrugged. "You're after the extortioners, after the people who threatened him, eh?"

"No, Cary, we're not." Desher's eyes were puzzled. "That's only the excuse we used to get into the case. The note was written on a typewriter that we found in the bank. But not a regular typewriter—not one of those in use every day. It's a *new* typewriter that was never supposed to have been used before."

Adair considered a moment. "Maybe he was framed by one of his subordinates? Maybe someone else got the money and framed him?"

Desher's face was grim. "And maybe Cossart is trying to make it look that way, Cary. That's just what I've been wondering. A dumb crook would have taken the money clean and tried to whitewash his tracks. No matter how far we progress in the science of deduction, these dumb crooks—no matter how 'bright' and 'clever' the average citizen may think them, they're dumb!—*they'd* try to cop the money and leave no trail. But a smart crook would leave a trail pointing to him, and then bring up the necessary alibi to absolve himself."

Adair shook his head. "I don't follow you, Jo."

"All right. Think this over: a man steals some money; he worries about getting away with it… always wondering if he's going to be caught. Suppose he works it in a clever way. Suppose he makes it look like a frame-up, then vindicates himself. The search moves elsewhere… and he is free—free in mind, free in body."

"Too *much* evidence, eh?" Adair nodded. "So you're going to check it and satisfy yourself on whether Cossart was just dumb, or smart? Or—a goat!"

"Something like that," Desher said. "But the minute we prove to ourselves that Cossart wrote that note… *if* he wrote it!… we're through with the case."

Adair sighed, leaned forward to crush out his cigarette. "So that's what is on your mind, eh, Jo? You think the F.B.I. is being drawn into this thing purposely, so that they can examine the matter, decide it's not for them, then get out permanently?"

Desher's eyes were grudgingly admiring. "You've hit it," he said. "My belief is, Cossart will turn up with the answers to everything. Despite the fingerprints on the securities… despite the bills in the safety deposit box… despite the note he never saw and that was written in his own bank and bears his fingerprints—my belief is, Cossart will be there with all the answers!"

Adair's eyes were skeptical. "Your *belief*, Jo? Are you telling me you just believe all this—right out of a clear sky?"

Desher shook his head. "Okay, Cary. I'll give you the rest of it: my field men up here have already checked on every fact. Cossart's coming out of this thing as clean as a hound's tooth, so far as we are concerned!"

"What? Despite the evidence against him?"

"Despite the evidence against him. Here's why. He claims—" The F.B.I. man broke off when Jeremy appeared again.

"A Bureau car is waiting, sir," the servant said.

Desher swarmed to his feet. "Well, Cary, I've got to go. I'll see you when I come back through on the way to Washington, if I can."

Adair jumped up quickly. "Why not let me ride up to Brayton with you, Jo? You know perfectly well you won't stop in on the way back."

The F.B.I. man grinned. "Come along, Cary. But I warn you, I travel at a speed that may jar your teeth a bit!"

Adair yawned. "Well... we've got to have a bit of excitement now and then, to whet the old appetite."

"You're telling me," Desher grunted. "I guess the last bit of excitement you had was clipping coupons from your bonds!" Jeremy gave them their hats soberly... but his lips fought against a smile as he opened the door for the F.B.I. chief and Cary Adair.

"Supper at the same time as usual, Jeremy," Adair said, as he went out into the foyer entrance and into his private elevator.

"Of course, sir," Jeremy murmured.

THE TWO friends made their way quickly to the Broadway exit of the great office building, Adair smiling quietly in answer to the greetings of the uniformed staff. A long, low, black limousine slid up to the entrance... a car whose official license plates were augmented by a plaque on which appeared the *D-J* that marked the vehicle as a Department of Justice automobile.

Adair's eyes took in the armored chariot with its bullet-proof body, shatter-proof glass with the slits for gun-muzzles, two-way radio, and the tear-gas bomb and gun case built into the rear of the front seat.

The car pulled away from the curb with a satiny mesh of gears and a throb of smooth power. Adair shook his head.

"This is one car that the ordinary citizen can't own, eh, Jo?"

The F.B.I. man nodded. "My mysterious friend Captain Satan is the only man I know who sports one identical to it. Some day, I hope to have the pleasure of relieving him of it."

Adair looked out the window at the traffic through which they slid, the magical *D-J* license and the moaning of the car's siren unsnarling the vehicular jams before them.

"But, Jo—your legendary Captain Satan… your ageless, matchless rival in the battle against crooks… his activities aren't bothering you, are they?"

Desher bit the tip off a cigar, lighted it and sank back into the cushioned seat. "God knows, I have occasion to be grateful to him, Cary. He's saved my life more than once. He has, in his mysterious way, picked up the scent of a half-dozen mad-dog mobs and cracked them, practically under my nose… cracked them and relieved them of their swag! He's the toughest one-man police force in the world. But he's barging into *my* business, and that's something I don't take from anybody."

Adair blinked. "From your accounts, Jo, he's cracked crime from the Bering Sea to the Equator. He's a tough cop who uses his brain and muscle to put the bad boys in the 'hot seat' and boil the sin out of their pores. You're hampered by certain state laws… but Satan steps where crime appears, and crime dies hard wherever he goes. Where's your complaint?"

Desher surrendered. "Unofficially, Cary, I have no complaint against Satan; except that the man has a nerve and a nose for crime and a trigger finger that I could use in the Bureau. Damn it, if I ever get my hands on him, I'll make him a proposition of 'Enlist with me or serve your time in Alcatraz!'"

Adair grunted. "A nice return for Satan's work, I must say. In one breath, you tell me he has practically filled Alcatraz for you, and in the next, you long to put him there yourself!"

"There's a properly constituted authority to deal with criminals. Satan isn't it. If he wants to help smash crime, let him join the proper forces constituted for that purpose," Desher retorted to his host.

Adair smiled. "Have you considered, Jo, that maybe Satan is the impatient type? Maybe he resents, *scorns* red tape—can't see the philosophy that dictates slow, orderly procedure that takes months—when *he* can go out and smash up the crooks without fear of a politically controlled police force screaming to Congress and High Heaven that it's un-Constitutional to smash a crook as you would a cootie—to smash him *when* he sees him and *where* he sees him? Have you thought of that, Jo?"

The F.B.I. man snorted. "You bet I have, Cary. And I'm jealous as hell! I go crazy when I see the rats that are hiding behind still rattier politicians." But the doggedness came back to his face again. "That's still my business, though... not Satan's!"

CHAPTER 2
BANK BUSTERS

THE F.B.I. car whirled through the city and flashed along the Westchester County parkways. The town of Brayton, a community of some 10,000 population, drowsed in the midsummer heat of the Hudson Valley.

The F.B.I. agent who chauffeured the car twisted down a tree-lined street and turned into the town's principal thoroughfare. Adjoining the west end of the railway station was a neat, compact, modern structure of two stories, built of gray stone.

Bank of Brayton, read the gold lettering on the wide windows.

On the cornerstone near which the car stopped were the Roman numerals MCMXXXVII.

"Nineteen thirty-seven," Adair deciphered the date. "Tough going for a new bank."

Desher nodded as he climbed down and walked rapidly to the side door. "A modern building… the latest electrical and mechanical devices to protect the money. And Cossart, its president, has a reputation of unimpeachable honesty for the forty years of his banking career. But the dough is gone just the same, my friend."

Inside, a dapper, alert-eyed youngster with blond hair and clean features saluted Desher with a smile and a handshake. "How are you, Inspector? I'm glad to see you again, sir."

Desher nodded and introduced the man to Adair. "This is Simmers, one of my best field agents." He turned to his subordinate. "Well? Did you break the case yet?"

"Belmann, of the Intra-State Mutual Banking Associates, is inside. There are two men from the bonding company, also. And the representatives of the State Banking Department, and the police. Calvin Cossart is in a bad hole; but he's taking it all pretty well."

"Hm," Desher considered a moment. "What about that note? The extortion note?"

"The fingerprints on the keys of the machine are Cossart's. No two ways about that. The paper is the same as that used in the bank."

The F.B.I. investigator nodded his head slowly. "So that's the

Captain Satan

end of the extortion, is it? There is no proof that the note had been mailed?"

"None," Simmers said. "The sheet wasn't even folded."

"Then the Treasury Department can't nose into the case on a charge of using the mails illegally. That lets us out—*if* the typing on the note matches the machine with Cossart's prints."

"And the typing does match."

Adair frowned. "You mean, Jo, that this washes you up with the case?"

"Right."

"But how about the money that was found in the safety deposit box?"

Simmers swung around. "Yes. What about that, sir?"

"That," said Desher, "is something for the state police to worry about. I expect Cossart will furnish alibis, once we're out of it."

"Cossart's own association is dead against him," Simmers said. "Belmann seems pretty upset. It seems that the Intra-State Mutual is a group of banks, banded together to promote certain features of banking. Savings Clubs, limited life insurance to depositors, and all the latest wrinkles. Belmann seems to feel that this may hurt the other banks in the group. He's barely civil to Cossart."

"I see." Desher scratched his chin. "What about the bonding outfit?"

"Cynically polite. They know they're on the hook. About all the State Banking Department is interested in is protecting the money of the depositors. The bonding company has to come across and do that."

"What about the police?"

"Cossart can't explain *any* of the fingerprints. Not those in the vault, nor on the securities that came in last week, nor on the threatening letter, nor the typewriter. They're taking him."

Adair nudged Desher. "Well, there goes your theory, Jo! You thought Cossart would be able to clear himself."

"Maybe he will, now that we're out of it," Desher grunted.

A door at the end of the hall where they stood swung open. A group of men came out. One of them, tall, severe-faced, primly proper but with a grimace of distaste on his wide thin mouth, stopped near Desher.

"Well, Inspector," he said crisply, "I imagine you've done all you can." But his voice and dark eyes said equally clearly that he didn't think Desher had done all he could.

A haggard, weary-eyed man of some sixty years glanced keenly at Adair and the F.B.I. men. He moved with the bewilderment of a man in a daze.

The severe man lingered after the others. "They're taking Cossart to the County Jail. He'll be arraigned to-morrow. Do you think he'll talk, when further pressure is put on him?"

"I have no idea, Belmann. I'm an investigator, not a fortune teller. What do you think? You've known him longer than I have."

"I've only known Mr. Cossart in the five years that I've been associated with the Intra-State Mutual," the man said slowly. "But even that short time seems to have been too long! Good day, gentlemen."

Desher shook his head. "This banking business is queer," he

murmured. "The decent ones seem to get into trouble; and the prissy, honest ones are sour as lemon balls." He turned.

"Well, Cary? Suppose we start for town again?"

"Right." Adair was starting out of the bank when a thought came to him. "Can you spare a minute, Jo? I want to pick up some etchings I ordered, on the way back to my apartment. I'd like to get a large bill changed, here."

"Step on it. The bank is closing down for the day."

Adair hustled to the large, interior banking room, whipped out his wallet, took out a hundred-dollar bill. "Would you mind changing this?" he asked the teller.

The clerk examined it closely, snapped it in his hands, stared at Adair. "How do you want it?"

"Oh... tens and twenties."

He picked up his change and was putting it into his wallet; but he paused, his eyes wide and startled. The teller stared. "Anything wrong, sir?"

Adair turned his gray eyes and looked at the man a moment, then went over the new bills slowly. "Er—no! No, thank you. I was just wondering about something." He started for the door.

"I was wondering," he muttered to himself, "what sort of a bank it is where the president writes himself a threatening note, the bank turns up seventy-five thousand dollars short—*and the tellers pass out brand new counterfeit bills!*"

He was glad that Desher was absorbed in his own affairs on the way to New York... because the puzzle intrigued him, the more he turned it over in his mind.

"...Bank presidents who threaten themselves... fortunes that

16

disappear… and tellers who pass counterfeit bills!"

Desher's parting with Adair at the big office building was abrupt.

"Good to have seen you, Cary. Take care of yourself." His face cracked in a fleeting grin, "And don't strain your muscles ripping the coupons off your bonds! 'By, feller."

ADAIR STOOD on the sidewalk for some minutes, his eyes thoughtful. Then he walked into a cigar store, thumbed through a telephone book.

"*Intra-State,*" he muttered, as he turned the pages. "*Intra-State Mutual Banking Associates…* Ah! Here it is."

The address it gave was only a few blocks up Broadway.

"It would be worth something to see old Belmann's glasses jump off his nose when I ask him to look over some of his own bank's dough," he murmured.

At the banking association's offices, he was greeted by a trim, petite and vivacious brunette. "I am Miss Pollarde," the girl said. "Is there someone you wish to see?"

Adair smiled. "Is Mr. Belmann back from Westchester yet?"

A voice interrupted from behind him… a voice that was smooth, suave, deep. Adair noticed that the girl, Miss Pollarde, shrank slightly and went back to her desk.

"How do you know Mr. Belmann is in Westchester County?" the voice had cut in. Adair swung around, his broad shoulders squared. A husky man with almost night-black hair and muddy-coffee eyes was staring at him.

Adair took him in quickly. "I saw him there, when I was with Desher, of the F.B.I. Why? Is it supposed to be a secret?"

The husky individual ignored the question. "Are you an F.B.I. agent?"

"No, I'm not." Adair met the man's gaze levelly. "Who are you, may I ask?"

"I'm Evans Arnleigh," the husky one said slowly. "I'm Mr. Belmann's assistant." He paused, stuck a cigarette into his hard mouth. "I suppose you're one of those nosey newspaper men, eh?"

Before Adair could answer, the outer door swung again and Belmann himself came slowly into the room. His eyes sought the assistant in a silent inquiry.

"A newspaper man," Evans Arnleigh said. Adair didn't deny the statement.

Belmann stared through his glasses. "Oh, I see. You—er— wanted a story on Mr. Cossart's arrest, I suppose? Sorry, but we are giving no information." He came closer, squinted slightly. "Don't I know your face?"

Adair shrugged. "I rode up with Desher, of the F.B.I. I was at Brayton, to-day." He whipped out his wallet, produced one of the overly-green twenties he had received from the teller of that bank. "I had occasion to change a bill there, I got this one, among others."

Belmann blinked and took it in his hand. Arnleigh came close. The manager of the Intra-State Mutual shook his head slowly, his eyes going back to Adair. "But, I don't understand you, Mr.—ah—what did you say your name was?"

But Arnleigh snatched the bill, held it in a better light. "Mr. Belmann! This twenty is a counterfeit! I'm sure of it!"

"So am I," Adair said calmly.

Belmann whispered, "What? A—a counterfeit? And he got it at the Brayton Bank?" He turned to Adair. "You'll swear to that? You can prove it?"

"I can only tell you that I got it from the teller in the first cage, near the side entrance."

"Ha!" Belmann stood in thought a moment. "It's a new bill, so I can't very well offer the excuse that the teller had come by it through an outside source and innocently passed it on."

"*It?*" Adair asked. "Maybe these will interest you, too." He took out the remainder of the bogus bills and passed them to Belmann. "I think you'll find they're all alike."

The bank association manager drew in a whistling breath and Arnleigh sighed. Belmann scanned the bills and shook his head slowly. "This is very serious, Arnleigh. Call the Treasury Department and report the matter. But wait a minute, please." He turned back to Adair. "When did you first notice that you had counterfeit money? Did you suggest to the teller that the bills looked queer?"

"No, I said nothing," Adair told the man. "I saw that they were phonies the moment I laid eyes on them. I—er—have seen one or two bits of counterfeit before."

A silence fell over the small room. Belmann and Arnleigh

stared at Adair steadily for a long moment. It was the assistant who broke the silence.

"Odd that you didn't mention it to Desher, my friend." His voice was quietly accusing. "What was your reason for that?"

"Counterfeiting doesn't concern the F.B.I., does it? Besides—" Adair shrugged, his gray eyes frank, "I sense some connection between the embezzlement and the passing of the bad bills. I'm... curious."

Belmann nodded quickly. "It means Cossart's gone bad in a big way!"

Adair agreed. "And it means the Government is back in the case... when you report this matter to the Treasury Department. I have a little matter of a hundred dollars sunk into this fraud, whatever it is, and I'd like to know that the affair is in the right hands." He smiled.

Belmann gestured with a hand and Arnleigh left. Adair heard him calling from another room. The manager spoke suddenly.

"Tell me—did you have a feeling that you were being followed after you left the bank?"

Adair blinked. "I never considered it. Why?"

"I was just wondering. If the teller knew these bills were bogus, thought you recognized the fact and kept it to yourself, he might have followed you; or have had you followed."

Adair laughed slightly. "I don't think anyone would be apt to track an F.B.I. car through the streets, do you? Besides, wouldn't the man, or men, reason that I was with Desher, and either an F.B.I. agent, or a man likely to *tell* Desher?"

"Yes," Belmann nodded. "And that's what I still don't understand, sir—why you didn't mention it to Desher instantly." He stirred and came closer. "And I have yet to hear your name, sir. What paper do you represent?"

The girl spoke from her desk. "Maybe he's looking for a scoop, Mr. Belmann. Maybe he wants an exclusive story!"

The manager turned and riveted an icy glare on the girl. "I don't recall asking for your opinion, Pam." He turned back to Adair. "If you print a word of this, sir, you realize that you may wreck that bank—may cause irreparable loss to thousands of depositors?"

Adair laughed and shook his head. "I promise you I shall not report it to a newspaper, Mr. Belmann. It just struck me that— well, I thought you'd get quite a start. *My* interest is in seeing justice done."

"Justice… to whom?"

Adair looked his surprise. "To the depositors and to the public in general, of course."

Belmann shrugged sourly. "I thought you were suggesting that Cossart was being unfairly treated, because of the fact that he has not confessed as yet."

Arnleigh came in from the other room. "May I have your name?" he asked Adair. "A treasury department agent will be here at ten in the morning."

Adair smiled. "So will I." He turned on his heel, waved cheerfully to the girl, Pam Pollarde, and stepped out into the hall.

CHAPTER 3
SATAN GOES TO WORK

ADAIR HAD threaded his way through three blocks of milling, homeward-bound workers when he was impelled to stop and turn suddenly. Two men stepped behind a parked automobile at the curb, but did not re-appear in the street.

"Hm," Adair grunted. "So, Belmann had the right hunch. I *am* being shadowed!"

He turned and started down Broadway again, his mind busy with the thing. "Someone who saw me examining that money at the bank is gambling that I haven't spoken to Desher. Or someone thinks that my knowledge and possession of the bogus bills is dangerous!"

He quickened his pace, crossed the street, rounded a corner. Abruptly, he wheeled in his tracks and started back again. He halted near the corner of a cigar store. Two men, hurrying in his erstwhile tracks, were on him before they could stop. One of them tried to break for it, but Adair's hand tightened on his sleeve like a vise. The other jammed his hand inside his jacket.

Moving with swift decision, Adair slammed his free hand to that wrist, jerked at it, brought out that hand that clutched an ugly automatic. The man's swarthy face went gray; but he fought to see it through.

Adair saw that he had no choice, that it was his own life or the other man's. He gritted his teeth with the effort, turned that hand until the gun pointed back at the man, then jerked hard. There was a crash of gunfire that lay flat in the still air.

Someone nearby screamed, and feet pounded along the pavement. Adair's other assailant made a supreme effort and wrenched away. Adair was after him in a flash, but the man had sped into the street, was running for an automobile. A burst of orange flame spurted from the rear window of the car. Adair dropped to the asphalt street and rolled quickly out of range.

When he came to his feet again, the car had ripped around a corner and was out of sight.

Crowds were gathering, and the siren of a police car screamed nearby. A uniformed policeman ran up, was stooping over the fallen gunner. Adair brushed his clothes off. Someone plucked at his sleeve.

"Hey! Aren't you the guy them hoods was after?"

Adair blinked, made up his mind instantly. "I? Hell, no! Those two were fighting between themselves. One of them pulled me along as a shield. I don't know anything about it." He moved into the gathering throng leisurely, seized his opportunity to melt through the milling masses.

ADAIR RE-READ the article in the next morning's newspaper that told of the gun fight on lower Broadway.

Lower Broadway was the scene of a brief but deadly gun fight between a member of a vaunted underworld gang and an unknown assailant.

Gink Lammartey, member of the sought-after but apparently vanished bank-cracking mobsters of Ted Krantz, was found shot to death by his own weapon after a brief struggle with an unrecognized gunster. In the spectacular duel, an unidentified pedestrian was imperilled when the killer made his escape in a waiting car that threw hot lead to discourage pursuit.

Adair put the paper down and frowned. "Ted Krantz," he murmured. "Ted Krantz... the 'Public Enemy Number One'

Slim

who dropped out of bank cracking when the F.B.I. came into the field!"

"Hm!" He rubbed his chin reflectively and stared at Jeremy. "Now just where does Ted Krantz fit into this?… into this hodge-podge of crooked bankers, embezzlement and counterfeiting? Why should *he* attack me, unless—" He broke off, his eyes alight with pin-points of excitement.

"—Unless Krantz has devised some modern method of robbery that keeps him under cover while he stuffs his pockets with his ill-gotten gains!"

He was still puzzling with the thing when he rapped on the door of the Intra-State Mutual Bankers Association at ten o'clock. The comely secretary welcomed Adair with a smile that crinkled her nose.

"We have some news for you," she said brightly. "The Treasury people came quite early this morning. They telephoned to Brayton, and that teller has disappeared! He must have sensed your suspicions and become alarmed!"

Adair pursed his lips thoughtfully. "And the counterfeit money?"

"The Treasury people took it. They said it was the work of a man named—named—" she paused, her pretty face perplexed. "Could it have been 'Raffles?'" Adair smiled. "It could have been most anything. But I doubt that it was the famous crook of fiction… Raffles!"

"Well, it was something *like* Raffles. Maybe it was… Raphael?"

Adair's eyes widened suddenly. *"What? Raphael Gartano?*

The master counterfeiter who dropped out of sight a number of years ago?"

"That's the name," Pam Pollarde nodded vigorously. "But the men who were here called him 'Raphael,' mostly."

"His nickname," Adair recounted slowly, his eyes shining with excitement. "After Raphael, the great Italian painter... because Gartano is a great painter, himself—a *painter* of bogus bills!"

The door of an inner office opened and Belmann stood on the threshold, his cold eyes taking in Adair. "The Mutual owes you thanks, sir," he said, coming across the room. He took out an envelope, passed it to Adair. "A hundred dollars in bona fide bills is there—*and* an additional hundred, for your thoughtfulness in bringing this matter to our attention."

Adair opened the envelope, counted out a hundred dollars, and returned the rest of it. "I'd rather have had one of Raphael's pieces for a souvenir than your generous, but unacceptable, reward."

Belmann bit his lip. "I hope you won't speak of this matter to anyone," he murmured. His eyes were hard. "The Treasury people asked us not to tell outsiders." His gaze slid around to pin on the Pollarde girl, then came back slowly.

"The teller has disappeared. His record is being checked."

"And what of Calvin Cossart? Are they questioning him about any connection there may be in this thing?"

"My friend," Belmann said slowly, "I wish to compliment you on your keenness of perception. It is apparent that Mr. Cossart is implicated in more ways than in just the embezzlement."

"Yes." Adair stood in silent thought. "It must be a blow to

any reputable banking group to learn that one of their member banks is involved in the passing of counterfeit bills." He mused to himself, *"Belmann is taking it pretty hard... but with a stiff upper lip."*

The assistant, Evans Arnleigh, came into the room. He stopped when he saw Adair, turned back toward his office.

"Miss Pollarde," he called. "I have a few letters to dictate."

Adair saw the grimace of distaste with which the girl received the summons; but she got to her feet, walked slowly into the inner room.

"You'll keep this quiet?" Belmann asked, his eyes steady.

Adair nodded. "Of course." He shook his head, wonderingly. "Funny—that Raphael Gartano and Ted Krantz's mob should both come alive at the same moment... and in the same case."

Belmann started. "What? Krantz, the old-time cracksman? Why do you link his name in this?"

Slowly, Adair told his story. The association man shrugged. "I saw the article in the newspaper," he said. "But, of course, I didn't link that shooting with you. Have you reported it to the authorities?"

"No," Adair said. "I've had a bellyful of this thing already. I'm a man who has a respect for law and order, Mr. Belmann—but I draw the line when the fireworks get too hot!"

"You're wise, as well as observing," Belmann said quietly. "I am glad you told me this, sir. I shall make it my business to report it to the Treasury officials. Good day... and, thank you again!"

ADAIR WENT out onto the street, his mind grappling with what he had learned. "Raphael—and Ted Krantz—and Cossart!

27

It would be interesting to know just how Cossart would react if he was faced with this development. I can't imagine how a respected, conservative, country banker like him came to be involved with Raphael and Krantz."

He was starting down the street again when the shouted "Wuxtry!" of a newsboy dragged his feet around. He signaled the howling youth, bought a paper.

Adair's eyes went narrow when he saw the headline:

ACCUSED BANKER SUICIDE IN CELL.

His eyes swept the scare-head, dropped to the triple-column sub-head.

Calvin Cossart Takes Hydrocyanic Acid Smuggled Into His Cell In Food Sent By An Unknown Friend Or Relative... it elaborated further.

Adair folded the paper abruptly and hurried to his penthouse.

"Pack, Jeremy," he ordered crisply. "I'm going on a short—ah—trip until this mystery is cleared up. There's more here than meets the eye!"

There was suppressed excitement in the manservant's eyes as he wheeled and disappeared into the pantry. "Immediately, sir," his trained voice answered. Adair walked to the studio window and stared out over the lower bay.

"Cossart is beyond any jurisdiction now," he mused. "But the great Raphael and Ted Krantz are breaking out of their retirement or I'm making a pretty sour guess!"

CHAPTER 4
SATAN'S CREW

I N THE musty air of an East River warehouse, a flicker of light sprang alive, speared through the darkness and stopped with its ray outlining eight masked men who stood against a far wall.

Slightly in front and at one side was a gaunt, lean-faced man whose masked eyes shone animal-like in the severe light of the lamp. Behind the figures lined at the wall loomed a black silhouette of a horned-figure with pitchfork upraised in a threatening attitude, as if to plunge down on those figures below.

"Ah, Slim," a cool voice came from behind the source of that spot of light. "I see you have the crew all here."

"Right, Captain."

There was silence for a moment, then it was broken by that cold, authoritative voice.

"Checked and identified?"

"Right, Captain. Fingerprinted, emergency call letters asked and given. Everything regular, Captain."

"Good. Start a Satan lamp, Slim. I want to have a talk with the boys before we make our first move."

The gaunt man picked up a large lantern, whose lens was in the top, and snapped the switch alive. An eerie glow of bluish-red light spread through the room, recoiled from the heavily matted windows of the place, searched into the darkest corners and lighted them softly but clearly. In the center of the lens was that same Satanic device… horned head, hand grasping an upraised pitchfork in horrible threat.

And into the light grew the figure of the newcomer… of Captain Satan, Nemesis of the underworld and racket-cracker extraordinary. More than six feet in height he stood, clad in severely dark clothes, a black tie and black shirt completing his costume. His feet were cased in light but tough leather shoes with crepe-rubber soles.

The black silk mask that hid his identity, could not hide the clean-cut features below. The eyes that gazed through the slits of the mask were twin specks of gray fire. When he moved, as he did now to come nearer the still figures against the wall, his muscles rippled under the light jacket that he wore… black in color, but light and snug-fitting. There was no excess of material there for a clawing hand to grip and stay the catlike movements of Captain Satan.

He braced, now, on columns of legs whose bulging muscle might have been hidden had he worn looser, more convention- ally clothes.

"How are you, men?" he asked, halting a scant few feet from those other masked figures. He shed his snap-brim hat, reveal- ing reddish hair trimmed close to his well-shaped head. His ears were flat above muscular, browned jaws. A strong pillar of a neck turned as his eyes went slowly down the line of masked faces.

"How are you, Cap'n," came the answering chorus. All hats came off.

"Just in case you might have forgotten," Satan said easily, his strong, white teeth flashing in his wide mouth as he spoke, "for what purpose are the men of Satan's Crew gathered here to-night… or *any* night?"

"To smash crime and crooks," came the solemnly intoned answer from the assembled men. "To defend to the death our brothers in the order and to preserve the secret of our identities at all times."

"Right," Satan nodded. "And—to relieve the crooks of their money, but to return to rightful owners any and all money that we can trace or identify as having been extorted or stolen." His eyes sought out a long-beaked, thin man in the group… a man whose eyes moved like busy little animals and sparkled blue in the light. A smile eased Satan's grim face.

"And to keep for ourselves what we can rightfully claim is impossible to identify. Isn't that right, Solly?"

"Oi, *oi!*" the eagle-beaked man said. "The take has been fine, but you look only at me, Cap'n! If only you shouldn't be so particular with your remarks!"

Soft laughter eased the tenseness of Satan's crew.

Satan got their attention again with a small movement of his head. "We'll check call letters, first. I can't impress on you men too seriously the importance of using your emergency letters when needed to identify yourselves to others of the group. I'll check you on them as I call your names."

31

"Right, Cap'n," came from seven of the eight. But one voice said, *"Captain."*

Satan's eyes were instantly alert. His hand crept to his tie, fingered it slightly. "Who said that? Who said... *'Captain?'* "

A slight, yellow-skinned man stepped forward, his black eyes blinking through the slits of his mask. *"I*—said... Captain."

Slim stepped forward, made a slight, saluting gesture. "The new member, Captain," he said. "Because of your haste, I've already inducted him in the various steps—up to the final one."

"Oh." Satan's eyes traveled slowly over the small man in front of him. "Who vouches for this man?"

A tall, debonaire, mustached man stepped forward two paces. "I do, Cap'n. I call him... 'The Chink.' Absolutely trustworthy. Small, but an accomplished wrestler, fast as light, can work a dozen disguises in as many minutes... almost. College graduate, professor of electrical engineering at one of our better universities."

Satan nodded slowly. "You're Chinese?"

"Yes, Captain."

Satan shook his head, but his voice was patient. "Only one man in this crew calls me 'Captain.' That's Slim... my lieutenant. The rest of you use the shorter form—'Cap'n.'"

The diminutive Oriental cocked his head slightly. "Is it permitted to ask why, Cap'n?"

"All you men come from various walks of civilian life," Satan said. "Not one of you knows who the other man really is... other than his name as used in the crew. Slim is no different. He, too, has a different station in life than that of my assistant—and an expert at palming papers or objects that we need from under the watching eyes of our opposition." He stirred. "But, in civilian life, Slim is in a position where polite deference is required. I keep him in training by making him call me 'Captain,' not as a weapon to demean him or to hold him down. But merely as protection for Slim himself, and for me."

'The Chink' nodded. "I... see. Slim is your subordinate in other life."

SATAN'S VOICE went hard. "We don't discuss those things, here. Now—you understand that you may be called upon to lay down your life? You know that you must obey my orders, or Slim's orders, without hesitation? Even though it mean your death?"

The Chink nodded. "I understand, Cap'n."

"Okay. Now—your call letters?"

"C-K," the man answered promptly.

"Right." Satan stepped forward, shook the man's hand warmly and smiled broadly. "I'm glad to have you with us, Chink. You've been proposed by one of the best men I've ever known, especially in the face of danger."

"Thanks, Cap'n." Gentleman Dan's teeth showed in a dazzling smile. "Call letters, G-D," he recited, as he shook hands.

"What? The emergency-call letters are the first and last of each name!"

"That's correct, Captain," Slim spoke up. "If we used 'D-N,' as we did once, it would clash with The Dutchman's. Gentleman Dan's are G-D."

"I remember," Satan nodded. His eyes traveled the group,

picked out a tall, stout blond man with cheerful blue eyes. "How are you, Dutchman?"

"D-N," the man answered briefly, shaking hands. Satan smiled. "In order, now… the rest of you. Make it fast."

Satan's Crew came on in a file, shaking hands, announcing the formula letters that they used in a crisis… when gang guns were blazing and mistaken identity could mean instant death for one of the crew.

"P-T." A red-mustached, stocky, broad man with bright blue eyes… a typical 'copper' type. Satan grinned. "'Lo, Pat."

"K-O." A broad-beamed, swarthy, flat-nosed man with curly hair that was black as tar. The crew leader chuckled. "Are you still a good driver and pilot, Kayo?"

"The best," the big man answered. "A regular Greek Barney Oldfield!"

"S-Y." A bald, furtive-mannered, pale-eyed chap shambled forward. "Glad to see you, Soapy," Satan said. "I think you're going to be busy on this trip!"

"D-C." A small, stooped, gray-haired man stepped forward, his blue eyes calm, deep. Satan slapped the man on the back. "Doc! Good to see you." He looked around. "Well? We're all set? Seats, men! On the floor. You all read the newspapers. I know that. I'll start by saying that I'm almighty interested in a current headliner that we can call 'The Affair at the Bank of Brayton.'"

The men dropped in a tight circle, but Satan remained standing, his eyes taking them all in. "I'll give you the facts, swiftly, so we'll all be thinking down the same track. Attention, please—

and if any of you don't understand the setup as I explain, just stop me."

He started his recital of the facts… and the alleged facts… of the embezzlement at the Bank of Brayton.

WHEN SATAN had concluded his sketch of the situation, there was a heavy silence. It was broken, at last, by the new member… The Chink.

"Cap'n? A tree that has grown straight for many years does not suddenly become crooked!"

Satan looked at the little man. "Meaning Calvin Cossart, eh? There are exceptions to that rule, Chink. Men have gone straight for years, only to fall for some wild scheme, or for some scheming girl, in the later years of their life. But I'm agreed with you on Cossart."

The Chink nodded slowly, soberly, like some masked Buddha. "A man who schemes to rob himself has time to scheme cleverly. He does not leave his marks wherever he goes. Man who has time to rob his own bank has time to do so leisurely… and to leave no prints after him."

"You'll do," Satan said, smiling. "Now, I still may be mistaken, men. Cossart, after all, may have robbed himself; may have left evidence that pointed to him and that he could, cleverly, have refuted. But such a man doesn't commit suicide when he is jailed."

Gentleman Dan raised his good-looking head. "It was on the level, Cap'n. Cossart was in it, right up to his neck. He saw a chance for a clean-up, and went after it."

"That's your theory? Then where do Raphael Gartano and

Ted Krantz fit into the picture? Krantz, the 'mad-dog' of gang-dom; and Raphael, the biggest counterfeiter of any day? Are they in the small-time game now?"

Pat pulled at his red mustachios. "That Krantz is a bad one," he said. "I pretty near had him, once—when he took the U.S. Mail trucks for a cool two millions."

"And he pretty near had me, yesterday! All right, men—ready for assignments." Slim whipped out a pad and pencil and made notes as Satan spoke.

"Gentleman Dan: Get around to the hot-spots, the night clubs, that big-time racketeers frequent. Keep your ears open for any mention of Krantz, or Gartano.

"You, Soapy—contact the stool pigeons and pay for any lowdown that's worthwhile.

"Solly and Chink, you're both electrical wizards. Find out just how modern the Bank of Brayton's alarm system is. Check the type of vault, if you can, and get the lowdown on that—if it's a time lock, and all the rest of it.

"You, Doc… I think your standing in the profession would enable you to find out how Cossart died, and when. Whether the hydrocyanic was taken with a meal, and whatever else you can uncover.

"Dutchman? You go up to Brayton and shop around. See if you can find any ten or twenty-dollar bills that look good, but are too green.

"Pat? I want you to get me copies of fingerprints of every one of the Raphael counterfeit mob and of the Krantz gang.

"Kayo? You'll drive me, as usual. Slim will stay with me. You men get your jobs cleaned up in a rush and report back to your telephones. Slim has your addresses and numbers. He'll call you for your reports, or summon you, in the event we need you. I'm going to check the Brayton end of it myself, tomorrow." He turned to Slim.

"Pass out the money, Slim. Also, the guns and the new tommy-packs."

Gentleman Dan stirred. "Wouldn't it save Slim time if you let us have our guns, to keep? Then you wouldn't be bothered with checking them in and out all the time."

Satan shook his head emphatically. "Absolutely not! You know my views on that. Every gun in this wide land should be registered. When one is sold, a ballistics test should be made first, and the 'fingerprints' of the gun should be filed along with the fingerprints of the man to whom it is sold. If that were done, half the crooks in this country would turn straight, or at least quit their murdering tactics." He looked around at all of them.

"I trust you men, each and every one of you! But we're going to play the law just as we think it ought to be played. I use these guns as a necessity to smash the crooks. But when that's over, they go out of service. All right, Slim, get going!"

A LONG, black car glided away from the deep shadows and sped west through a deserted street. Minutes after the purr of its skid-proof and puncture-proof tires had died on the still air, two shadows detached themselves from the adjacent blackness near where that car had been parked, and went quickly down the street.

In the swiftly gliding car, Satan leaned forward and snapped a two-way radio set alive. In a moment, the voice of a popular news-caster was coming to him and Slim. They had unmasked, as had Kayo, the driver. The husky chauffeur was sitting with his eyes stiffly ahead of him, not even glancing into the rear-view mirror. Satan, sitting in the dark corner on the right of the rear seat, sat straight suddenly and listened to the broadcast.

"...A queer parallel to the embezzlement at the Bank of Brayton was apparent in the State Banking Department's admission, late tonight, of a sixty-thousand dollar shortage at the Saugerville Bank, at Saugerville, New York, a small community near Poughkeepsie....

"...Seth G. Saugers, member of an old and respected family of that section and a descendant of the founder of the town, was under arrest tonight after evidence pointing to his guilt had been uncovered....

"Rumor has it that Saugers attempted suicide after his arrest, and is in a critical condition."

The announcer signed off.

"My God," Satan breathed. "Saugerville! Why, it's only a town of... well, no larger than Brayton!" He punched a signal bell, spoke tersely to Kayo. "Head for Saugerville, Kayo. We'll stop somewhere this side of it. I want to be there when the bank opens in the morning." He swung to Slim.

"How's that for a shock? Two bank presidents, in what are practically neighboring communities, embezzle funds from their banks... both are men who have enjoyed the best of reputations... and both leave tracks that involve them!"

Slim shook his head. "It's too much of a coincidence." He thought for a moment. "But, Captain? Maybe it's just as it looks. Maybe these two men just *did* need the money, saw their chances and grabbed it, were clumsy enough to leave their signatures around on the stuff."

"It could be that," Satan admitted. "But it's funny that it happens just when Krantz and Raphael stick their noses above ground for the first time in years!"

The car turned north on the Hudson River Drive and stretched its long-nosed hood for the environs of Poughkeepsie.

CHAPTER 5
VOICE OF THE GUN

S ATAN WALKED slowly down the shady side of the main street of Saugerville, his eyes seemingly casual but missing no detail of the bank that stood in the shade of the elevated railroad trestle and depot.

It was a small but substantial and gleaming white building of late design. Satan stopped at a drug store, looked briefly at his reflection in one of the window posts.

In his severe black clothes and dark, bone-rimmed spectacles, he appeared to be a serious-minded student or professor rather than the toughest 'private cop' in the country. His eyes rested a moment on the clock... the clock that marked the hour as approaching ten.

As in most small communities, the bank had opened at about 8:30; but Satan had spied the F.B.I. car in front of the door, had

seen men who wore the worried
expressions of public officials
hustling in and out of the place.

In the local paper, he had
already conned the news of the
arrest of Saugers, the bank's president, and of his reported attempt
at suicide, by hanging, in the cell
of the Poughkeepsie jail where he
had been lodged to await arraign-
ment. He had puzzled at the similarity to the Brayton embezzlement... had listened, as he ate a light breakfast, to the aroused
citizens discuss that same feature.

"Only natural," one shrewd country man had observed.
"Crooks work pretty much alike the world over."

Another said, "Shucks! Like as not ol' man Cossart give
Saugers the idee. Seems like it's a bad 'un, if they try to kill
themselves after stealin' the money."

But about one feature Satan was intensely curious. "If any
queer money turns up here, Slim, it's any odds you care to name
that I'm on the right track... and that Raphael, the counterfeiter, is in this thing deep! You wait in the store across from
the bank. Kayo has the car down at the depot, just in case we
have any reason to step fast out of here. I'll nose into the bank
when the track's clear."

And, now that the track was clear... the F.B.I. men and the
State Police and the banking officials had departed... Satan
crossed over to the bank. As he was about to enter, he saw a man

who had been standing on the steps peer at him keenly and walk rapidly away. Satan frowned but kept on his way.

The bank was a thoroughly modern institution, with the officers sitting behind a polished mahogany rail and the tellers caged in their glass fronts. And off to one side was a flat, desk-like shelf of marble that ran back to a neatly furnished section marked by a sign, *Ladies Department.*

Satan took his place in line behind several others and waited with a crisp hundred-dollar bill in hand. He noted the tenseness of the junior officers, where they sat behind the rail—judged the fear in their eyes as they saw the more-than-average run of depositors who were filing in, bankbooks in hand.

"Afraid of a run," Satan realized. "Well, it's only natural they would be. There's no place like a small town to fan a rumor into a blaze of certainty!"

It came his turn, and he moved to the window. "I find I have no small bills," he told the teller, with a smile. "Would you mind changing this for me?"

The youngster, dark-haired and blue-eyed, looked at it. "Of course, I'll be glad to change it. How will you have it?"

"Tens and twenties."

A grim line etched Satan's mouth when he saw the bills that were being counted out for him… bills that were crisp and new but that had, to his expert eye, that same tinge of too-bright green that he had detected in the Brayton currency. His keen eyes swept the other bills, the orderly stacks of them that were behind that counter, and it dawned on him that as far as this

41

teller was concerned, the money he was passing out probably seemed perfect in every respect.

Because all the other bills in sight were of the same color!

A dozen possibilities built themselves in his mind as he put his hand out for the money. He stood to one side, apparently counting, but in reality watching the man behind him present a check and draw out money… money identical to that which Satan had received… money that was counterfeit beyond a doubt!

"Tradesmen… business men, large and small… housewives— *all* are getting up on line for their share of the queer money!" he thought. But in the next moment he tried to laugh at the sheer daring of the thing… or at his too-lively imagination.

He tried to laugh—but he choked it off when he saw five men start up the steps of the bank, slowly, calmly… but with that "savvy" of the seasoned veteran about them. It flashed through his brain that they were coppers… Treasury men, maybe; but he overruled that when he saw the hard, tough faces of the men, their glittering, evil eyes. One of the five stopped abruptly at the top step, wheeled and stood athwart the open door.

Another posted himself just inside the doorway, his eyes ranging the crowd. The other three moved in quiet but drilled precision, one of them coming directly to the teller's window, another stepping close to where the officers of the bank were seated. The remaining one walking calmly to the flat-topped marble shelf and put his hand lightly on it.

"Okay!" the man at the door snapped, as his eyes took in the positions of the various members of his party.

And a tommy-gun bloomed in his hand from under his topcoat—as if by magic.

"Hold it, everybody! Down on your faces," the man at the teller's window blared. "This is a stick-up!"

SATAN HURLED himself under the mahogany rail near at hand and rolled behind a desk. He came up on his knees, his hand whisking a .45 out of the cleverly concealed shoulder holster that he wore.

A racking chatter of machine-gun fire broke horribly in the small building. Satan saw the rain of plaster that showered down from the roof and realized that the man at the door was spraying the place with lead to put the fear of God into the people.

He crouched, his gun at ready, and peered around the desk. The man at the teller's window had the muzzle of a sub-machine gun jammed through the bars. Another was vaulting the marble rail, was scooping stacks of bills into a bag that he had produced from under his jacket.

Satan whirled back, took careful aim at the machine gunner in the doorway. He pressed his shoulder against the desk to steady himself and squeezed his trigger finger carefully. Two shots crashed close to the leg of one of the junior officers; but they found their mark in the man at the door. The gunner staggered, fell back against the jamb of the door, slid to the floor with his mouth gaping, his eyes glazed, and blood pouring from his shattered head and brain.

Firing started from near the cages. Satan turned, taking advantage of the cover of the desk, saw the thug with the black bag scaling the low fence. Satan aimed quickly but accurately, pumped two bullets into the man's body while he was still in mid-air, in the act of hurdling the obstacle. The gangster crashed to the floor and skidded into a paralyzed customer, bringing him down in a heap atop his lifeless body.

A nearby explosion tore a huge sliver from Satan's shielding desk. The crew leader felt a wave of dizziness go over him as a bit of burning lead creased his skull, knocking his hat off. He remembered the man who had stood guarding the officers in the inclosure, snaked under the desk as he saw a pair of feet creep forward.

He knew he couldn't wait for a shot at a vital spot, opened fire on those exposed feet and ankles. There was a scream of pain, and suddenly feet pattered across the bank floor. Satan saw a hand swoop down and snatch the black bag that the fallen thug had dropped. He took a quick shot—but knew that he had missed.

Hoarse shouts came... then the sound of running feet, and another blast of machine-gun fire. Outside, an automobile motor raced. The shooting broke out anew as gears meshed loudly and a car roared down the thoroughfare.

The stick-up was over, but the gang had left two dead behind them, while a trail of bright red blood showed where a third had dragged his smashed underpinning across the floor in a superhuman effort.

Satan came out of his hiding, jamming his gun back into its holster. "Please sit still, everybody," he called loudly. "I'm—I'm an officer. Just hold your positions where you are, until we make sure these other two hold-up men are *really* dead!"

He stepped quickly across to the man at the doorway, bent to pluck the tommy-gun from his hand…but halted in his tracks, his eyes wide with astonishment.

A cut-out device, made of cardboard and colored with great imagination, was lying in the center of the bank's floor.

And that device was the Satanic head, with pitchfork upraised in a threatening gesture!

Down the street, a siren rose on the air. The voices of excited citizens were shouting and calling out. The people in the bank stirred, coming out of their shocked lethargy. With a shake of his head in exasperation and annoyance, Satan veered away from the front door, walked quickly for the side entrance.

HE STEPPED out, rounded the corner of the bank as a police car screamed to a stop and disgorged its horde of uniformed men. Taking advantage of the wild confusion, Satan started down the street for the depot. Slim came from the store and walked parallel with him, but on the other side.

Townsfolk were running from all directions. Slim crossed over. Satan said, "Kayo will know enough to drag back to where we spent the night, if we don't show up. Follow me."

The two men turned near the railroad station, walked down the tracks when they neared some stationary box-cars. Satan skirted behind one, saw that the door was open, climbed in and helped Slim up. He shut the door carefully and stood staring wide-eyed at his lieutenant.

"As fine a stick-up as was made in the best style of Ted Krantz," he said slowly. "And as coolly and matter-of-fact as the notorious Jesse James himself."

Slim shook his head. "All I saw of it was a gunner on the steps standing as calm as you please, machine gun in the crook of his elbow, staring down at the driver of the car. The driver had the motor going but he had another tommy-gun draped out the window, on his side."

"How long do you think it took? About three minutes?"

"Less than that. I'd say—" Slim paused, his eyes judicious, "I'd say just over two minutes. From start to finish."

Satan agreed. "It seemed longer to me, naturally. But the experts never take more than two and a half minutes… though some frightened bystanders will assure you that the shooting was going on for a full hour."

"What do you make of it, Captain? What mob do you think it was?

"Krantz! Krantz from start to finish! That's his technique, that man at the door methodically spraying the ceiling, while the others just go to work. I got two of them… but that won't help me much, when the F.B.I. gets on the job."

Slim was puzzled. "What do you mean? How can it hurt you with them?"

Satan's eyes were heavy with speculation and regret. "The F.B.I. will be in on the game as soon as one of that Krantz mob is identified. They don't even need that! Krantz's methods are as clear and distinct as a set of fingerprints."

"But if the F.B.I. does jump in, how will they connect you with it?"

"Because," Satan explained slowly, "those gunners came

outfitted with a Satan emblem, and they very nicely dropped it on the floor of the bank. That's how I'm implicated!"

"My God!" Slim stared. "How do you account for that? Is Krantz trying to pull his stuff and tack the blame onto you?"

"No, I don't think it's that." He stirred, gestured with his right hand. "I suspect that Krantz is in it, don't I? And that in some way Raphael Gartano is in the deal, too, with his phony money. I stood there and *saw* it being passed out, and took some of it along with me."

"Yes?"

"So if Krantz is trying to frame me in the thing, trying to make it look as if I had a hand in it—*then he must know that I'm on his trail!*"

"But, how could he know?"

Satan shrugged. "I can't answer that one... until I catch up with Krantz. And then he'll answer it, not I! But, Slim; one of my pet theories is going into the discards, unless I can figure out the weird angle of this thing. If Krantz and Gartano are operating together, as I believe, then why does Krantz spend two of his men and leave both his trademark and mine—*to grab off a bundle of queer dough?*"

Slim scratched his head. "This thing is crazy," he breathed. "Just crazy!"

"Sometimes, Slim, genius appears to be merely insanity," Satan said. "But brilliant or crazy, I'm going after that gang that cracked down here today. When night comes, get the boys and bring them up here. Meanwhile, I'm going to tour the back roads and map what I think would be the most logical cooling spot—the most likely hide-out—that this gang would pick!"

CHAPTER 6
SATAN CLOSES IN

S LIM BOUND Satan's creased scalp with a handker-chief, then scouted the depot for signs of Kayo. But the burly driver had evidently tooled the car out of the place after the uproar had died down. Slim reported back to the box car. Satan said:

"Kayo probably went back to where we spent the night. We'll split in a few minutes. I'm going to see if I can trace the general direction taken by those hoods, and figure out about where they'd have staked out their cooling spot. You call Kayo, and give him orders to stay at the farmhouse until night. Then, get in touch with the crew and have them meet near the little white church just before the cross road, at the farmhouse."

"Right, Captain."

"After that, I want you to track through Saugerville and see if you can locate any bills that look like these." He fished out his wallet and handed Slim some tens and twenties. "Meet me back at the farmhouse at about dinnertime."

"You'll be all right, Captain? Sure you don't want me along?"

"Can't spare you from this other work," Satan said. "I'll dig down to the next town and rent a car that I can drive around in."

After Slim had left, Satan busied himself with cleaning up his face and hands, using the mirror of the small washing kit he carried in his hip pocket. He brushed his clothes off, straightened out the wrinkles in his hat, and when the coast was clear he slid down from his place of hiding.

At a garage two miles south of Saugerville, he produced an operator's license and a bill of large denomination.

"I'm looking over some property in the neighborhood," he said to the man in charge. "Can you rent me an automobile, if I leave a large enough deposit?"

The man whistled at sight of the hundred-dollar bill. "Name your car," he said, pointing to a row of them. Satan selected a small coupé of popular make and filled the tank with gas. He twisted the wheel to nose the car for Saugervile, and slid his bone glasses into his pocket as he came to the outskirts of the town.

He drove slowly, setting the trip-mileage indicator of the speedometer to *000.0*. As he came past the bank, he pushed the register pin in, and swung the wheel. The instrument started to record the mileage from that point, in miles and tenths-of-miles. A steady stream of people were filing past the bank, staring curiously at the windows of the place, and at the stream of dried blood that crossed the sidewalk.

At the railroad intersection, Satan slowed, saw a cut-off to the left that led away from the main road. "That would be *my* turnoff," he reasoned. He pulled a pad from his pocket, wrote in pencil:

0.9: TL—end.

"Turn left, nine-tenths of a mile, follow to end," he judged.

He drove along slowly, saw the marks of tires where brakes

had been slammed on hurriedly. The road reached about two miles, then dead-ended at a T-road. Satan reasoned, "A left turn would bring them back onto the main road at Saugerville. They must turn to the right, here." He wrote it down... reading the mileage. *2.9 miles... TR.*

Some five miles down that road, signs of a small settlement ahead showed in roadside advertisements of gas, oil and a restau-

Joe Desher

rant stand. A small red schoolhouse on the left marked a road intersection that led to the left again. Satan paused, pondered the thing. "Did they all remain in that car they were driving at the bank? Or—did they have confederates, girls, probably, waiting down the road so they could split into two or more cars and thus avoid any net thrown out by the State troopers?"

He was about to drive on to the garage advertised ahead when he saw a white something at the side of the road, down to the left. He wheeled his coupé into the narrow road and pulled to a stop. He jumped down, saw what it was that attracted his attention—

A white handkerchief, with still-damp splotches of blood on it! Satan wrote down *7.5 miles TL red schoolhouse*.

HE DROVE down the road, slowed still more when he came to a small bridge. He pulled to a stop and climbed out. There was a slight bump at the head of the bridge, a roughness in the road that wouldn't be noticed unless a car was travelling at high speed.

Satan clucked his tongue in satisfaction. Skid marks appeared on the bridge and in the dirt on the other side. A car, travelling at high speed, would make just such a mark as this. He drove on through the woods country, stopped at a field gate some seven miles on. It was a crude fence, with the conventional two bars of wood. But the bottom one was out of place… was resting on the ground. Satan walked over to the gate and looked at the stubblegrass beyond it. Twin tracks showed where a heavy vehicle had crossed not long before.

Satan marked, *15.6 miles, through fence into field and woods*.

He let down the bars, drove the car through the fence, put the bars in place again. Through a twisting woods road, he went, his eyes careful on the rutted path before him. He came to another gate, examined the narrow lane, frowned when he saw the tracks of wheels that twisted to the left… and back toward Saugerville.

"Hm," he mused. "A hideout can be anywhere from close in to eight hundred miles away. But—I never heard of one *this* close… unless it couldn't be handled any other way."

He drove to the left, marking, *16.2 miles. LT through fence.*

Three miles onward, he came to a rambling, apparently deserted farmhouse on the left side of the road. He kept his eyes strictly on the path ahead of him as he went, came to wilder country that dead-ended, so far as the road was concerned, at a small slope of land. But the wheel marks had stopped back near that farmhouse.

Satan swung his coupé around and drove back; rapidly, this time. He passed the abandoned farmhouse, whizzed by the gate in the field where he had crossed and drove on for a few miles. The lane led into a state road. Satan got down at a gas station and asked for a map of that section of the state. He snapped it open, stared knowingly at the criss-cross of state roads that hemmed in the sector he had travelled.

"Pretty bold," he murmured, shaking his head. "The cops probably reason this mob put lots of mileage between the cooling joint and Saugerville. But—it would be dangerous for them to try, with this honeycomb of main roads they'd have to cross and re-cross; unless they split up into other cars with their molls as camouflage."

He drove back to where he had rented the car, skirting

Saugerville as he went. "On the other hand, it would be smart for them to lay out a decoy track to a logical cooling joint...where they could seemingly be waiting for the heat to die down... and all the time actually jumping for a hiding place hundreds of miles away."

He had more than a hunch that he was right, though...knew that with a wounded man in the car, the mob couldn't risk detection by carrying him along the highways.

When he reached the garage, he paid his bill and walked slowly down the road. He stopped at a telephone station and rang the number of the farmhouse. He asked for Slim, using the alias they had decided on.

"The car's here," his lieutenant reported. "I've been in touch with—ah—our *friends*. Everything is set, following your instructions."

"Good," Satan said. "I'll get a taxi around here and drive down there. As soon as it's dark, you go down to the white church and get the reports. I'll want a few of the crew with me... tonight. The rest can wait for orders."

IT WAS two hours after dark when Satan stepped from the white blob that was the side of the church house and whistled two low, penetrating notes. An answering whistle came from the carriage shed over at the side. Satan's light flashed swiftly over the masked group that stood there.

He walked swiftly through the gloom and stopped under the cover of the ancient vehicle shed. "Slim?"

"Yes, Captain?"

"All present?"

"All but Pat, Captain. He's getting the Raphael and Krantz mobs' prints."

"Give me the news. What did they uncover?"

The group stood silent while Slim answered slowly, fully. "Gentleman Dan reports that there are rumors of a heavy floating of phony cash in the hot night clubs. Tens and twenties are coming in for plenty of close inspection. One man told him he had it on the level that a half-million dollars was being floated."

"Sounds possible," Satan said. "What else?"

"Soapy bought some information from two stool pigeons: One of Ted Krantz's old gunners left town last week—evidently got some work. And a former bill-poster of Raphael's is griping that there's a new wrinkle on that's cutting him out of his usual take."

"What? A bill-poster? You mean, a passer of counterfeit money?"

"That's it, Captain. The Dutchman found plenty of queer cash in Brayton, but when he complained of one bill in particular, the tradesman swore that the money was okay because he'd got it from his bank."

Satan was silent a moment. Then: "Solly? What did you and The Chink dig up?"

One of the group moved in the dark. "Cap'n!—I'm telling you that Edison himself couldn't escape the electrical alarms that they have in the Brayton Bank. Time combinations… double electric set-ups, so if the town power fails they got their own working… the walls of the bank and all the windows wired. Oi, such a seestem!"

Satan nodded. "You agree, Chink?"

"The system is very clever," the little Oriental said. "But—if a man makes a system, a man can also break the system."

"What do you mean by that?"

"I mean, where there is much money at stake, great brains will fight to get at it. One brain makes a clever system to protect it, but other brains will work to destroy it This system is very good, however."

"Doc? How about Cossart's suicide?"

"He took enough hydrocyanic to kill a regiment. But—here's a funny thing, Cap'n… Cossart was highly nervous, and right after someone sent him a hot dinner, a specialist from New York called to examine him. He was with him some time, and when he left he warned the police at Brayton to keep a close eye on the banker. Said he feared suicidal tendencies."

"So Cossart took the easy way out?"

"Not to my way of thinking, Cap'n. Cossart had a permit for a gun, had several at his home and in his office. He could have done the job much better that way than with hydrocyanic. But—here's the trick part of it: just to close the record, the cops tried to fingerprint the glass the acid had been in. There were acid traces in the water, all right… but not a single print, Cossart's or any other, could be found on the glass!"

"Hm. Maybe—Mrs. Cossart sent the doctor and the dinner,

eh? Better check on the medico, and see why he thought Cossart was going to kill himself, and just what the police did about guarding him from it."

Doc's voice was mild when he answered; but there was a world of meaning in it. "Mrs. Cossart was under a doctor's care herself, at the time. She sent no dinner… she sent no doctor… and when the police looked in on Cossart's cell, right after the specialist had left, he was apparently sleeping. He—never moved from that position! And the police didn't have the doctor's name."

Satan started. "It… looks sort of odd, doesn't it, Doc?"

"Sort of," the medico admitted. "There are plenty of possibilities."

The crew leader thought a moment. Then: "Suppose you go over to the county seat and find out what you can about Sauger's condition? *He* tried suicide, yesterday."

"Right, Cap'n."

"Report back to your station in New York. The rest of you… all but Gentleman Dan, Slim and Kayo—and you, too, Chink and Dutchman—go back to New York. Chink will go to Saugerville and check on any phony money he can dig up there. Gentleman Dan, Kayo, Dutchman, Slim and I have a little errand to perform."

CHAPTER 7
WHEN A RAT SPEAKS

KAYO AND Gentleman Dan sat on the front seat of the limousine that rolled slowly down the main street of

Saugerville, and turned right at the bank. The husky driver held a sheet of paper in his right hand a moment, ran his eyes down the column of abbreviations and numerals.

0.9	*TL—end.*
2.9	*miles… TR.*
7.5	*TL red schoolhouse.*
15.6	*TL through fence in woods.*
16.2	*TL through fence in road.*
19.7	*miles to farmhouse on left.*

"You'd think the Cap'n rode with those guys," the swarthy driver muttered. He started to push the visor of his hat up, remembered his orders to keep his features obscured as much as possible. The signal buzzer sounded loudly in his ear.

"Yes, Cap'n?" Kayo spoke into the small box-tube at his side.

"Keep your eyes on the road," Satan snapped. "Kill your lights when you come to the first fence marked on that getaway chart, and keep them off. Step on it, now."

The black car stepped fast under Kayo's expert guidance. The big fellow grinned slightly and shook his head in admiration as the various changes of direction clicked off on his speedometer… exact to the fraction.

When the car turned into the narrow road near the schoolhouse, Satan signaled to Slim, who leaned forward and pressed a hidden spring, then pulled the hidden door of the front seat open. Arranged in neat, specially-designed clamps were several tommy-guns, tear gas bombs, a sawed-off shot gun fitted with pistol grips, and a quartet of .45 automatics.

Satan signaled with his buzzer when they were through the first fence. "Masks," he ordered tersely. The lights were snapped off and the car crept along the narrow road. He slammed the brakes on suddenly. There was a fence just ahead. Gentleman Dan stepped down and loosed the bars. The car turned left down the road.

With a half mile yet to go, Satan gave orders for the car to be turned around and headed in the opposite direction. Then the quartet took the guns assigned them and went into the field for a stealthy approach on the old, abandoned farm. Satan whispered an order to halt when the grove of trees they tracked through came to an abrupt end. In the denseness ahead they could see the outline of the old buildings.

Slim took Kayo by the arm and led him to the rear of the house. Satan motioned to Gentleman Dan to stand at one side. When Slim'd had time to get to the opposite side, Satan went silently to the front of the house. He stooped low, skirted around the front, knelt on the damp ground.

There was no sound from within, no sign of light nor of life at all. Satan crept to the porch rail, found a post that was firm. Quickly he yanked a coil of steel cable from his pocket and made it fast to the upright. He crossed over the steps quickly and fastened the other end securely, forming an invisible barrier that was about a foot above the top step. He crept back silently to where Gentleman Dan was.

"Open up with your tommy-gun on the rear of the house… upstairs and down. But get behind a tree. If there's anyone there, they'll open up at your muzzle flame. Now—count ten and open fire."

Satan dusted back to where he could observe those front steps. He had dropped to a squatting position on the ground, tommy-gun in hand, when the racket of machine-gun fire broke the stillness of the night.

Gentleman Dan ripped more than a hundred bursts into the house, with no answer. Then, from Slim's post, came another smash of firing. The bullets that Slim poured into the house started at the middle of the place and ate forward. Kayo's gun joined the uproar, spilling lead into the back windows.

Still no answer from the house.

Satan stood, pulled two tear-gas bombs from his pocket, hurled them at the glass upstairs that glinted in the light of the orange-red flames. There was a tinkling of shattered panes as one of Satan's missiles found a mark. Instantly, two jets of red streamed from another window. Satan paused as the machine-gun fire broke out in the rear of the house again.

The front door slammed back suddenly, and feet thudded across the porch. There was a loud twang as a foot caught in that taut cable, a wild curse, a body crashing down the steps. Satan sped forward, saw a dark form moving on the ground, smashed his clubbed gun down on the knob end of it. There was a groan as the form collapsed.

Another man ran out and came hurtling down the steps. But he landed on his knees, slid a few feet, came up with his gun blazing. Satan raised his lethal weapon and fired. A scream of pain rang out, and the gunner crashed down to the ground.

Grimly, Satan stood and hurled still another gas bomb into the blackly yawning doorway. There was a curse of fear, a sudden crashing of gun fire. In the rear of the house, a glass broke and twinkled in pieces.

Krantz

Belmann

Raphael

Satan blasted a leaden hail into the doorway. From inside came a shouted, "K-O! K-O!"

Satan ceased firing. There was the sound of heavy bodies crashing inside. He ran lightly up the steps, hurdling the cable, and slid into the doorway. The grunting of men and the thud of

Kayo

Chink

Ezra Timkens

heavy bodies came from a room on the left. Satan snapped his pocket flash alive and thrust it into the room.

In the spotlight stood a heavy, masked man in the act of raising a wriggling figure in his great arms. High above his head, he raised the struggler, then smashed him heavily to the floor. The breath went out of the man in a painful gasp, but Kayo… no mean wrestler in any ring… was on him like a terrier after a rat. Up and over his head again, he raised the gunner, and slammed him down hard. He landed beside another still form.

This time, there was no movement.

"That does it," Satan snapped. "Take the stairs, carefully. There may be more of them up above." He went down the hall, met Slim and Gentleman Dan coming in the back way. "You, Dan— fire a blast down the cellar stairs, and follow it up. Slim—you search the back rooms. I'm going to have a look in the woods on the other side of the house. I have an idea their car might be hidden there."

SATAN WAS back in five minutes, watched Slim and Kayo carry a wounded man down the stairs. He came close, saw the crudely bandaged feet. "That's the one who creased me. I shot him in the feet and ankles. Load him out into his own car. I found it… brought it up in back." He paused. "Any sign of the dough? In a black bag?"

Slim shook his head. Satan looked closely at the man in the dim light made by Slim's flash. He saw the slight shine on the man's eyes as he peered through slit lids.

"Where's that dough, gunner?"

There was no answer. Satan waited a long moment. "Okay,

men. Put him down there on the floor and we'll get one of his pals in here, see if we can make sense out of this."

The men Kayo had knocked out were dragged into the hall. Gentleman Dan came up from the cellar, a black bag in his hand. "Here's something, Cap'n."

Satan grunted, dropped to his knees, tore the bag open. He trained his light on the bills that were there, looked them over carefully. He got to his feet again. "It's all queer dough," he said, slowly. "I don't get this... Ted Krantz's mobsters raiding a bank for queer money."

The wounded man cursed long and heartily. Satan laughed. "You didn't know the dumb play you were making, eh? Just think it over, mug! You got yourself lined up for a long stretch, got your feet shot up, too... for jumping a load of phony money. And yet you crooks think you're smart!"

"You're a liar," the man rasped.

"Hold him up, so he can see," Satan told Slim. He yanked some of the bills out and held them close to the man. A hard light followed the amazement that had come into the bandit's eyes.

"Okay, buddy," he said through tight lips. "I don't know what's behind this thing; but you can bet your last nickel that Teddy Krantz will wish he was in hell when I pass the word around."

"What word?"

"Listen, buddy—don't try to kid me! You're smart enough to know that we don't touch no bank that ain't been fingered right. Not on'y that—but we even had directions on which size bills to grab. There's a double-cross in this pile somewheres, an' it's going to end up right on Teddy Krantz's forehead… *cut* there!"

The unconscious men were brought in from outside. Slim brought them around with a whiff of ammonia from his first-aid kit. He showed the men the bills, let them see what they had fallen for. Then:

"Spill it, now. Where is Krantz? When did he come out of hiding? Where's he operating from?"

There was no answer. Satan's face was hard in the lamp light. "Kayo? Just put a little pressure on these mugs. They'll sing, or I'll see that every bone in their bodies is cracked!"

Kayo jerked one man erect, twisted his arm savagely behind his back. "Ya rat," the man sobbed, when the pressure racked him with pain. "Ya dirty rat!"

"Listen to who's talking," Satan laughed. "A big, tough guy that hijacks with machine guns, who shoots innocent people down in cold blood… and now he's calling us rats!" His face was forbidding. "A little more moxie on that twist, Kayo."

The gunman screamed and then babbled pleadingly, "Chees, cut it out, will ya? I'll talk. I'll talk!"

"Start talking," Satan snapped. "And make it fast. Where is Krantz?"

"Somewhere in New Joisey," the man whispered. "I—I don't know where. He ain't in the picture, in the blasting, I mean. He toined a crew of us onto this job, said it'd been fingered right an' was ready for th' can opener."

"When did Krantz come back into the business? How did you get your orders?"

"He—" the man paused, whimpered. "I'll get me tongue cut out if I tell ya. I don't peep to no hijacking crooks, and lose me tongue."

"You won't live to feel the pain of it, if you don't," Satan snapped. "Do you talk?"

"I—talk," the man broke. "Teddy's been lyin' low for five years or so. We got our orders through Tough Tommy Maddlin—the guy who was killed at th' door o' th' bank. He's one o' Teddy's regulars. We wuz out o' work, an' he give us a chance."

"How about this mug with his feet shot?"

"He—he was a regular o' Teddy's. But, neither him nor me has seen Teddy in years, now. Honest, we got it straight through Maddlin."

"Where'd you hang out, in the city."

"I ain't from the city."

"Kayo? Give him another massage!"

"No! No! Chees, I'll tell. Down at Texas Twomey's joint, on th' East Side."

Satan swung on his heel. "That settles it! This man is a liar, he couldn't even get into Twomey's club. That's a pretty high class place. Kayo—drag in that lad I conked with my tommy-gun. We'll just give this gang a going over with it, and leave them all here. Step fast!"

THE THREE men were silent—but impressed—when Satan's masked men dragged in the now conscious gunner, then stood them all against the wall. Satan lifted his tommy-gun casually.

"I gave you your chance," he said slowly. "But—you didn't

want it. I wanted to know your hangout, and you lied. I also wanted to know who's idea it was to drop that Satan trademark on the floor of the bank—but that can wait, too. I'll get the lowdown from Krantz himself."

He held the gun in plain view, then raised it slowly. The man with the wounded feet got to his knees, croaked, "Shoot them. But lay off me. I'll talk!"

Satan smiled grimly. "Well! Where is this honor among thieves? I thought you lads never squealed, never sang? Hurry up and talk!"

"Okay. Our hangout was at Ollie Uppers, over on the riverfront. The orders was to drop that Satan trademark. That came from Tom Maddlin. It seems this Satan rat is onto Krantz, in some way, and we wuz to leave him a warning and get him in wrong with the Sams at the same time."

Satan's voice was flinty. "Who are you calling a rat?"

"Huh? I said, Satan was a—" The man paused, his eyes going wide. "My God! You! You're—?"

The men stood there against the wall, and suddenly, as the man jerked out his unfinished question, Satan took his cigarette lighter out of his pocket with his free hand, reversed the small affair, and pressed the button. Instantly, the wall in back of the men was illumined by the weird light—in the center of which was the satanic figure, pitchfork upraised. The four men, one on his knees, cowered as the crew leader spoke softly.

"I'm Captain Satan," he said. "I'm going to smash the rest of Teddy Krantz's mob just the way I've smashed you. Now, where does Raphael Gartano fit into this picture? Raphael—the queer-dough king?"

One of the other mobsters stirred. "That's screwy. Raphael and Teddy aren't mixed. If Teddy was interested in the queer dough, what would he be doing cracking banks for the real McCoy?"

Satan's smile fixed on the man and the gangster started suddenly. "Say! We *did* jump a bank, and came *out* with queer dough. Now, how in hell did that dough *get into* the bank?"

"When I know the answer to that," Satan said quietly, "Raphael and Krantz are going to sit in the Hot Seat—as guests of honor!" He turned to Slim. "Bundle these rats into their own car, money and all. Drive them up to our car, handcuff them, and we'll park them on the road for the coppers to pick up. This is one load of bank blasters that are through with their work for a long time to come!"

Slim moved forward. "I've got a set of cuffs on me," he said.

"Give them to me!" Satan took the things, snapped the shackles on the toughest of the lot, the gorilla that he'd smashed with his gun when he catapulted down the steps. Then he went out, untied the steel cable, rolled it and jammed it into his hip pocket. GENTLEMAN DAN took the wheel of the gunners' car and drove it from where they had parked Satan's car to the main road. Then, with the lights flaring across the darkened road, he stripped the necktie off one of the mobsters and tied the horn of the mob car so it would sound incessantly. Then he departed in his own car.

The signal shrieked through the night as Satan's car doubled

back in its tracks and made for the
getaway route over which they had
come.

"One thing's sure," Satan said,
as they fled through the field and
turned onto the schoolhouse road.
"In some way, we were tracked by
Krantz. We'll drop the old meeting place and hop to the new one,
over on the Hudson River side."

He snapped the radio on, unmasked, and sat back with a cigarette between his lips. The car had covered half the distance to
New York when a flash announcement came over the air.

*State Troopers north of Saugerville, scene of the bank robbery that
followed close on President Sanger's embezzlement of sixty thousand dollars, were attracted to an automobile with its horn blowing
raucously.*

*Four shackled men, said to be members of the notorious Ted Krantz
gang, were apprehended. The men would not talk, but it is strongly
held that there is a gang war going on in the underworld… a war
which took its toll of two men of the Krantz gang to-day.*

Slim blinked when the announcer broke into talk on another
subject. "They never mentioned the phony money," he said.

Satan kicked a bag that rested at his feet. "I decided not to
leave it with them. Whatever this thing is, it's closely tied up
with the counterfeiting racket of Raphael's. The F.B.I. is in this
already; and Belmann notified the Treasury Department of the

bogus bills at the Brayton Bank. If they hop this job too, and it becomes public, Raphael may be scared off."

The car was tooling down the deserted West Side drive when another announcement came in:

Gaynor Belmann, of the Intra-State Mutual Bankers Association, has asked an investigation into the Saugerville Bank robbery by the Federal Government. Attorney-General Claxton is opposing this bitterly, on the grounds that it is State and not Federal business.

Belmann says that this second of his group of banks that has figured in notoriety in the past two days requires that immediate steps be taken to track down the guilty parties. News of the capture of the Krantz gang had not reached him at the time the announcement was made. It is said that the bonding company covering the embezzlement is trying ineffectually to get a statement from Seth G. Saugers, who continues in a critical state.

Saugers attempted suicide by hanging shortly after his arrest.

"My God," Satan breathed. "Another Intra-State bank!" He sat straight, his eyes narrowed. "I think we'd better call on Belmann in the morning and give him some inkling of the truth at Saugerville! Maybe the two of us, working this out together, can get someplace!"

Slim stirred. "Don't forget that we're implicated in this, Captain! If, for any reason, we were suspected, or happened to barge in while the F.B.I. or Treasury agents were there, it might mean almost anything."

"We can guard against that," Satan smiled. "We'll make it a point to get there when only the office force will be at the

Intra-State. As to recognition—I imagine we can take care of that, too!"

"The new meeting place, to-morrow night," Satan gave instructions, as he and Slim quit the car on lower Broadway and climbed into a taxi.

CHAPTER 8
TIME FOR ACTION

S ATAN STEPPED out of the telephone booth and walked to the cigar store door. He motioned Slim to follow him as he turned up the street. Satan, clad in a yellow polo coat and with bone-rimmed glasses that were visible below the peak of his cap, was turned out like a conservative sportsman with a touch of the Britisher about him.

Slim was tall, gaunt, severe in chauffeur's garb, had just the proper tinge of deferential respect about him to carry off the picture of a servant.

"Belmann's secretary answered the telephone," Satan said. "Belmann and his assistant are in conference and can't be disturbed, she says. No appointment possible this afternoon, because Mr. Belmann has to be in Saugerville at that time."

"You gave a name?"

"No. Just said I was motoring and found something that I thought would interest him. I said I'd call again tomorrow. Let's get right up there before anyone else barges in."

At the offices of the Intra-State Mutual, Slim let Satan go first, following respectfully and with his cap in his hand.

Belmann's secretary got up and came over. "Is there something I can do for you, sir?"

Satan smiled; but he didn't remove his cap. "I'd like to see Mr. Belmann," he said. "It's a personal matter—and one that is very important to him."

The girl frowned. "Mr. Belmann can't be disturbed," she murmured. "Is it anything that I can do?"

Satan shook his head. "No. I'm afraid not. I just wanted to tell Mr. Belmann that I found the money that was stolen from the Saugerville Bank, yesterday."

The girl gasped. She walked quickly to a door and knocked. "I can't be disturbed," came a high, imperious voice. "I thought I made that clear, Miss Pollarde?"

"But there's a man—"

"I don't care. Send him away. I'm busy."

Satan walked slowly to the door, turned the knob, pushed it open. Slim walked casually after him, his eyes taking in the details of the place. Inside, Belmann sat behind a large desk, his face hard and his eyes glittering behind his glasses. He had the desk drawer open. At his side was his assistant, Evans Arnleigh.

"Sorry to be so insistent," Satan said mildly. "I believe I have found the money that was stolen from the Saugerville Bank, and naturally I didn't care to turn it over to anyone else but you. May I come in?"

Belmann sat silent for a full minute, his eyes widening slowly. The assistant came to his feet silently. But neither man spoke. Satan smiled and asked, "Quite a surprise, eh? I don't wonder you're astonished. Now, Mr. Belmann—how about giving me ten minutes of your time to discuss this thing?"

Arnleigh strained his thick neck out from his shoulders and pursed his lips. "Discuss what?"

Satan blinked and stared at the man. "It isn't an every-day occurance to have a bundle of money brought into your office from the highways, is it, sir? That's what I wanted to discuss."

Belmann stirred. "I see. Well, have your chauffeur wait outside, please."

Satan shook his head. "It happens it was he who found the black bag, with the money in it."

"This is a small room," Belmann protested.

Satan's patience left his face. "Do you want that money turned back to the bank, or don't you? I'm not going to stand here and beg you to let me turn it over to you." He looked at Arnleigh. "It strikes me that if anyone has to go outside, it might as well be you."

Arnleigh's muddy eyes blinked slowly; but he didn't move. Belmann shrugged. "Very well. Come in, then, Mr.—? What might your name be?"

"It might be almost anything," Satan said, as Slim pulled the door closed. "I don't care to be involved in this matter; I can't spare the time. But, first—before we get to the money angle of it, there are a few questions I'd like to ask."

BELMANN WAS silent; but he motioned to Arnleigh to pull chairs close to the desk for Satan and Slim. The two men sat down, Satan first glancing at his casually disguised features in the mirror behind Belmann. He considered the association manager a moment. Then:

"If I'm not mistaken, this is the second of your banks to be involved in embezzlement, isn't it, Mr. Belmann?"

"*My* banks?" The man laughed slightly. "My dear man, I'm the manager of an association that works for the improvement of banking services. A sort of combined public relations counsel, advertising agency and purchasing agent. The financial structure of the bank is in no way my affair."

Satan smiled. "But—naturally you are interested in the reputations enjoyed by your banks?"

"As you say... *naturally*, I am."

Satan opened his coat, pulled out the black bag that contained the money he had wrested from the Krantz mob—the counterfeit bills—and opened it. He dumped the currency on the table, then checked it with a slip of paper he had in his pocket. "Fifty-three thousand, six-hundred seventy dollars," he said matter-of-factly. "If you'll count it and please sign a receipt for me—?"

Belmann reached for a receipt pad that was on his desk. But Arnleigh stepped up quickly and started counting. When he was satisfied that the amount was correct, he said to Belmann: "Okay. The amount is right. Now—shall I call Saugerville?"

"Yes. From the other office."

Satan waited until the man had gone, then said quietly. "Please add to that receipt, *In counterfeit currency.*"

Belmann's self control was magnificent He stared at Satan a moment, then reached for a packet of the bills. He examined them carefully, then picked up another packet. At length he said,

"This money did not come from the Saugerville Bank. Of that I am certain. Who are you, and how did you come by this money?"

Satan selected a cigarette from his case and puffed on it, exhaling a thick cloud of smoke. His eyes were busy appraising the man opposite him. He set the cigarette on a tray on the

The four men cowered as the crew leader spoke softly.

desk, watched the column of smoke rise in a straight line for the ceiling.

"I'm putting some of my cards on the table, Belmann," he said slowly. "But—not all of them. You might call me a private investigator. That's close to the truth. You have a strange situation here, in your banks. Two of them show mysterious embezzlements; two of them show up with counterfeit money. One of the presidents of the guilty banks is a suspected suicide, and the other is in a critical condition following an attempt to take his life. But there's more in this than meets the eye. I know for a fact that Ted Krantz and Raphael Gartano are mixed up in this. Why don't we face the facts frankly, and try to work together?"

Belmann leaned forward, his hands gripping the desk. Satan cocked his head slightly. From far away came what sounded like a subdued ringing of a buzzer. Belmann spoke, then:

"And we know for a fact, sir, that a certain Captain Satan is involved in this," he said. "Satan's mark was found on the floor of the bank at Saugerville, after the holdup. Do you still refuse to give me your name? Or would you rather tell it to the police?" His tone was ominous.

Satan's eyes narrowed. "Don't be a fool, Belmann! The F.B.I. men are in this thing only because the Krantz gang have been tracked through your bank. But they're in it! The Treasury men will be in on it as soon as they hear of that counterfeit money showing up in the bank. Raphael and Krantz will be scared off this job before you can lay a hand on them."

"Why aren't they scared off it now? What makes you think that they will continue active?"

"Because, in some way, they have a soft snap in these jobs. The alarm systems are perfect. The banks are crack-proof. The presidents and the tellers are apparently honest men. Yet—money is embezzled, counterfeit is passed through the cashier windows, and the teller at Brayton disappeared. If the game worked twice, it will work again!"

Belmann's eyes flickered slightly. The column of smoke that was drifting from Satan's cigarette to the ceiling eddied slightly, drawing the crew leader's eyes up.

"...Well," Belmann said, his voice slow and studied, "I have other banks to consider, of course. Now, if—" He paused, started to open his desk drawer again. Satan knew what was going to happen.

He put his hands on the desk and slammed himself backward, his hands going up and over his head. His fingers encountered a thatch of heavy hair, slid back and locked around a bull neck. With a mighty heave, Satan jerked down and jutted his shoulder up.

The burly form of Evans Arnleigh catapulted over his head, slammed across the desk and squarely into Belmann, knocking the manager and his chair to the floor with a resounding crash. Satan was on his feet in a flash, diving across the desk and landing on the two men. Arnleigh was struggling to raise a gun. Satan whipped out his own automatic and clubbed his wrist viciously. The husky assistant dropped his gun.

But Belmann was on it in a flash. He lifted it, fired point-blank at Satan. Hot powder seared Satan's cheek. The deafening crash of the gun stunned him, but only for a moment. He stuck out his foot, jammed Belmann's gun hand to the floor, held it there with all his weight.

Arnleigh was up, his eyes murderous. He swung a roaring hook for Satan's jaw; but it didn't connect. Satan ducked, brought his right hand up in a ripping uppercut that staggered the man back against the wall. Slim pushed Satan gently, cleared him of Belmann.

"I'll handle this lad," he said softly. And he was just in time. Arnleigh was charging again, had swung a straight right that stepped Satan back three feet. But when the burly assistant tried to follow it up, he walked into a rain of knuckles that battered him back, straightened him against the wall, dropped him, split-lipped and dazed, onto the carpet.

The door slammed open and the girl, Pam Pollarde, was in the room, her eyes wide with terror. "Wha—what's the matter?" she gasped. She let out an ear-piercing scream. But Satan reached out a hand and jerked her into the room, slamming the door.

"Hold it," he snapped. "I don't want to be rough with you, but if you let out another yell like that I'll have to gag you!"

SATAN LOOKED appraisingly at Arnleigh. "The next time you open a door to sneak up on a man, make sure that there's no cigarette smoke to show the new current of air." He gestured with his head. "And that mirror back of Belmann's desk shows a thing or two, when you're sitting in front of it."

Pam Pollarde sank down in a chair, her face ashen. Belmann's face went white when Slim yanked out a pair of handcuffs and pinioned his wrists behind his back.

"What's this? Are you calling the police?"

Satan laughed. "Hardly. We're trying to stop you from doing that. Do you think we're crazy?" He turned to Arnleigh again. "Frisk him, Slim. I'll keep an eye on Belmann."

Satan's lieutenant made fast work of the job. He uncovered a shoulder holster, a pack of cigarettes, a large quantity of bills of various denominations; but no other weapon. He went over to Belmann, found he had no weapon of any kind. He removed Arnleigh's belt and tied the battered man's arms behind him, at the elbows. He put a light gag on them both.

"The next time a man tries to give you a break, I'd advise you to be a little less jumpy," Satan told Belmann evenly. "Your judgment doesn't seem much better than your banks. I came here to try and help you."

Slim was putting something into his inside pocket when Satan looked around. "Disconnect the telephone, Slim. I can't chance anyone's kicking the instrument over and calling for help. Also, dig around for a key to this door. I want to—" He paused.

Slim had a key in his hand, was tossing it up and down as he listened.

"Where'd you get that? What is it?"

"Arnleigh's pocket," Slim said, his eyes owlish. "It looked like a fit." He walked over, tried it, nodded his satisfaction.

"I guess that's all," Satan said. He moved forward, shaking his head in regret. "Looks as if I've wasted time on this visit. Well—" he turned at the door. "A messenger will bring the key back to this building with instructions to release you, in thirty minutes, unless you're found before then," Satan told the men. His eyes slid to the girl. "Do I have to tie you, too? And gag you? I'd rather not."

"Oh, please, no," the secretary gasped. "I'll promise you anything, but please don't tie me. I'm—I'm too—*nervous!*" She shuddered and looked at Arnleigh.

Pam

Satan frowned. "I'll take your word that you'll be quiet." He turned and was gone, Slim locking the door after him.

The two men stopped at a telegraph office and left careful instructions with the clerk about bringing a certain key to a certain party at a certain office. "If no one is there," he repeated, "the key is to be turned over to the building manager." He left a generous tip for the messenger and went quickly down the street. Slim followed a slight distance in back, to make them less conspicuous.

Satan paused at a newsstand and purchased several late edition papers. He was turning away when a shouted, *"Wuxtry! Wuxtry! Read about the latest bank scandal!"* brought him around in his tracks.

He located the newsboy and paid him for the extra edition he was hawking. He went to a restaurant, dropped down at a table and ordered coffee. Slim, with a paper of his own to read, sat a little away from him.

THIRD BANK EMBEZZLEMENT BREAKS AS

SAUGERS DIES, the headline screamed. Satan ran his eyes down the thing quickly, taking in the details:

> Seth Saugers, embezzling up-state banker, died early this morning as a result of the slashing of his wrists and hanging, in his prison ward of the Poughkeepsie Hospital.
>
> At the same time reports came from the State Banking Department that a third bank in the neighborhood of New York City is under investigation. A shortage of eighty thousand dollars is charged. State banking officials are dazed by this third successive embezzlement. The newly accused official is Tobias Ellert, of the Midcity Bank, in Westchester county.

Satan downed his coffee, paid his bill and walked quickly out into the street. He followed Slim to where their small, rented car was parked.

"Drop this jallopy where we hired it. Meet me at the new headquarters as soon as you can. We've got to move fast on this or a bank panic such as has never been seen will sweep the State… the nation! Contact the men and get them over to the new place for orders."

Slim nodded; but he paused to yank a typed slip of paper from his pocket. "Midcity Bank, eh? No wonder Belmann was so jumpy. That's the third of his banks to go in three days!"

"What?" Satan stared. "How do you know that's another of his banks?"

Slim held out a sheet of paper. "I palmed this while I was frisking Belmann. I sort of thought it might be interesting. All I saw was the heading… *"New and Old Banks."*

Satan took the thing. "Hm. No reason why the man shouldn't have this record with him. After all, it's his business." He stared at the sheet. "That's funny, isn't it? There are asterisks… stars… after some of the bank names, and others are blank."

Slim looked over his shoulder. The sheet read:

BANK OF JONESVILLE.*
BANK OF LEATOWN.
BANK OF BRAYTON.*
JONESVILLE BANK.*
BANK OF TAYLOE CITY*
MIDCITY BANK.*
SAUGERVILLE BANK.*
HARRISSTOWN BANK.
SELKIRK BANK.

There were others; but Satan jammed the thing into his pocket. "We'll go over those names later," he said. "Right now, the important thing is speed and information and a little skull work for the crew. Step fast, Slim!"

CHAPTER 9
RAPHAEL'S ARTISTRY

S ATAN'S CREW was gathered in a warehouse on the West Side of New York. The crew leader stood at one side, scanning the masked men before him. Behind him was a big blackboard, with chalk and an eraser. Slim, masked like his leader and the men, turned and faced Satan.

"All present, Captain."

"Right, Slim." Satan faced the group. "Reports, men. Doc, I want yours first."

The slight, stooped medico stepped forward. "Saugers protested his innocence, Cap'n, and asked for his lawyer, a city man. Before long, a man appeared and presented his card, hustled in to see the prisoner. Saugers was pretty well thought of, up Poughkeepsie way. This is the first trouble he's ever had. They let him see his man privately, in the detention room. Saugers seemed to be nervous, so his lawyer suggested that he be taken back to his cell. He was. And they talked there. The guard came back forty minutes later. The lawyer had left, and Saugers was hanging by his neck from the cell door, with his wrists slashed."

"Ha!" Satan's eyes narrowed. "What's the lawyer's story?"

Doc shrugged. "That man wasn't the lawyer he said he was," the little, gray haired man said. "The lawyer Saugers had sent for showed up as they were taking the dying banker to the hospital."

"What?" Satan stood rock still. "But—he presented an identical calling card, at the jail?"

"The police are making an under-cover search for the man," Doc said. "I got next to the police surgeon and borrowed the calling card. It had a number of prints on it; but I developed all of them, just in case you were interested."

"Good! Turn them over to Pat, for checking with police records." He gazed down the line, nodded to the small, brown man in the group. "You, Chink? What did you find?"

The little man pulled some bills from his pocket. "Bad money at drug store. Bad money at candy store. Bad money at railroad station. Bad money at hotel." He shrugged. "Bad money all over."

Slim took the bills and ran through them quickly. "All phony, Captain." He stared again, intently. "Damned nice job, though—except for that over-greenness."

"And that wouldn't be noticed if everybody had crisp, new greenish bills," Satan pointed out. "You see, counterfeit money is generally 'washed' down, is soiled slightly so that its too-brightness will not be noticed. But—" He paused, his eyes puzzled. "I know it sounds crazy, but these bills all came from respected and trusted banks. The bills would *have* to be new, couldn't be washed down, to slip through the paying windows."

He looked around at his men, then went over to the blackboard.

"Now, we're in for a short skull session. I want every one of you men to give this your entire attention. First—I'm chalking down a list of coincidences in these embezzlements and queer-passings. Any of you think of them, sing them out. I'll write the first one:"

Satan chalked.

1. Queer money passed through both banks.

2. Both bank presidents involved in embezzlements.

Doc spoke up suddenly. "Cap'n? I went over the police reports on the Saugers case. They had him dead to rights, with fingerprints on some securities he had chiseled and put into his own private safe... and also, from the vaults of the place, where the money was kept."

Satan nodded. "So I understood. Well? How about it, you men?"

Gentleman Dan said, *"Three: Each embezzlement followed a rainy night."*

Satan stared. "What's that got to do with it? How do you know that, anyway, Dan?"

"Didn't I get my patent-leather shoes messed with mud enough to know that?"

Satan nodded. "Right." He said, "Next?"

4. Each was a recently built, new building, Solly supplied.

5. Both presidents dead, The Chink chipped in.

6. Amount of queer money picked up and amount embezzled come to approximately same figure as at the Saugerville Bank, Satan wrote.

Pat called out, "Say, Cap'n? Why hasn't there been any mention of the counterfeit bills in the newspapers. I ain't seen a word."

"Probably the Treasury people are keeping the muffler on it until they run down a few more leads," Satan said. "They ought to do plenty of shouting after Belmann hands in the queer money I left with him to-day. Well? Any more?"

7. No Federal money in either bank, blacking out the F.B.I., Slim suggested.

8. Each job has been done on successive days, The Dutchman said.

Satan's eyes slid to meet Slim's. "That's something to think about, considering that the Midcity Bank makes it three in a row. Suppose you slip out and get whatever quick information you can on that Midcity job. Telephone up there. Get information on the weather, ask if it is a new bank, check on anything you can, at this distance."

"Right, Captain."

While Slim was gone, Satan watched Pat look at the finger-prints that Doc had developed from the calling card the 'lawyer' had left with the Poughkeepsie police. He saw the stocky, red-haired man turn his masked eyes slowly from card to card. And he saw him start suddenly. Satan went over. "What is it, Pat?"

"I don't have to go to Headquarters for one of these prints," he said. "I got it right here—with the Raphael gang's. It's Dandy Joe Montori!"

Satan crossed to the board, noted: *9. Raphael and Krantz mobs working together.* As he finished, Slim was back. The lieutenant crossed over quickly and said to the crew leader, "The acid test proves it, Captain! It was raining last night in Midcity; the bank is new... built last year; Tobias Ellert, the president, had an extortion note hidden away in his desk—asking for Eighty Thousand!—and he left his prints on the bank vault and on the note. He denies ever having seen the paper, though!"

Satan sighed. He went to the board, added:

10. Extortion notes equal amount of embezzlement, in each case.

He looked at Slim significantly, then added his last notation of a pattern in the thing.

11. All three banks are members of Intra-State Mutual.

"Copy those items down, Slim. Then we'll wipe the board clean and do a little figuring on where we work next."

"Right, Captain."

THE AMBASSADOR FROM HELL

IT WAS a silent, alert-eyed group that Satan faced when the board had been mopped clear. His voice was crisp, and excitement shone in his gray eyes.

"Men… we are up against a modern Jesse James, a bank robber who has the daring and the cunning of James, plus a modern wrinkle of robbing banks from the inside. We've seen three banks go in three days. By breaking the thing down, we know that these rats are following a pattern… a pattern of involving the bank president, of killing him, of striking again with the speed and viciousness of a rattlesnake. Three banks in three days! What's next? Four in four days? Five in five days? Will every institution have to close down for a check to be made on it? Will the racketeers kill banking in the section they are tackling now? *They will unless we stop them!*"

He turned to Slim, snapping open a map. "Slim? Mark down the locations of the banks in the Intra-State group. Chart them on the board." He passed along the slip of paper with the list of banks, the paper that Slim had purloined from Belmann's pocket.

Slim did so, working fast. Satan took the list of banks, looked at it and at the stars that appeared after the names of some of them.

"Evidently, the asterisks mark the new banks," Satan said. "Mark them the same way on the map, Slim." When the chart had been completed, Satan studied it. After a moment, he turned.

"We have no reason to believe that a new bank will not go tomorrow; *to-night*, maybe! Our job is to figure *which* bank, and

87

to slam in and try to stop this gang—if the work hasn't already been done. I want every piece of scientific and fighting equipment that we can possibly use to be brought along. That goes for you, especially—Solly and Chink! I may want to go over that vault system myself, may want to test the wiring system. It's evident that this work is done *after* banking hours… most likely at night. If that's true, then the alarm system's a phony."

"How do we figure where to go?" Gentleman Dan asked, puzzled.

"I'm coming to that, Slim—mark down the towns where *new* banks that haven't been touched are located. They are all in a close group. Then, 'phone to those towns for local weather information. We'll follow this chart right through this time, and see if it works. If there's a new town where rain is falling, or likely to before the night is over—up we go! Pat? You have pretty good police connections. You go out and do that now. Slim will give you a list."

"Yes, sorr, Cap'n."

"Now, Slim," Satan ordered, "you're to give the police warning, at Midcity, without mentioning any names other than that of Tobias Ellert, that you fear his life may be attempted. Warn them to hold any man who represents himself to be a doctor, lawyer or friend. Get Midcity on the telephone now, and impress them with the importance of doing their best to guard Ellert."

"Right, Captain."

Fifteen minutes passed before both Pat and Slim were back again, with their masks adjusted. Slim reported, "Ellert is alive and yelling his head off for a lawyer. After what I told them, I don't think he'll get to see one... soon."

"Good. What about you, Pat?"

"I called all the towns you wanted, Cap'n. Clear weather for all, right now. But a local storm is gathering up at Tayloe City an' the coppers there think it'll rain plenty by nightfall."

"Okay," Satan decided. "Tayloe City is the spot! We'll give it a try. I'm going to shoot the works on this one. Slim? I want you to get the name of the president of the bank up there. Pick out your men to snatch him. If he's in on this mysterious racket, I'll want him! If, as is entirely possible, he is an innocent man, then I'll want him to question him about anything suspicious that may turn up."

"Right, Captain."

"I want every man-jack of this outfit to be in the vicinity of that bank by dark to-night—ready for action. Slim will pass out the guns and ammunition. Also, he'll appoint a meeting place, after he's cased the bank—in case we want you for further work after I'm through. But there's just one word of warning—"

His eyes were bleak as they traveled over his men.

"If you get into any mess with the police or Federal officers, you are to withhold firing at them, even if it means your capture. If any coppers cover you, break for it if you want. But—God help the man of mine who hurts one of the local, State or Federal men. Is that clear?"

"Yes, Cap'n," they answered in chorus.

"Okay. Slim will detail you men for the job of getting the president of the bank. Good luck!"

"Same to you, Cap'n."

Satan studied the blackboard carefully, while Slim called, "Dutchman? Gentleman Dan? You lads will get the president for us. Pat?—"

CHAPTER 10
DIRTY MONEY

S ATAN STOOD in the shadows and the protecting cover of a great tree, his eyes on the Bank of Tayloe City, several blocks down the tree-lined street. It was Saturday night; and like most suburban banks, the small, modern financial institution was re-opened from 7 to 9:30 o'clock for the deposits of tradespeople in the town.

There was still a half-hour until closing time.

Satan stiffened suddenly. A small, closed car which had passed the bank several times was cruising down the street again… cruising toward the tree under which Satan stood now. As it came under an arc light, the crew leader saw the silhouettes of two of the occupants looking back, toward the bank. The driver, his eyes straight ahead of him, was pulling to a stop.

For several minutes, the trio sat quiet, then one of the men opened the door, got down, crossed the street quickly. He had a small, square, dark package in his arms. He disappeared in back of the bank.

Satan stirred, peered into the shadows opposite—where he knew Slim was standing alert. He backed behind the tree, pulled a tiny flash light from his pocket, winked it alive three times, taking care that the men in that car couldn't see it. A moment later, an answering twinkle flashed from Slim's hiding place.

The man who had vanished in the gloom near the bank was coming across to the car again. Satan made an instant decision, came from under the tree in a staggering, rolling walk. "If I can get near enough to them to see who or what they are," he reasoned, "I'll be a step ahead in this game!"

Simulating a drunk, he lurched near the open door of the car, hiccuped loudly. "Shay, fellers! Any you guys got a light for a cigarette?"

The man entering the car stopped, his head snapping around. Beady, alert eyes stared into Satan's. "G'wan, ya lush! Scram outa here before ya get chilled."

"Climb in!" the driver snapped to the man on the running board. "We got to lam. This business o' wiring the wilds don't include chin sessions with lushes." Three sets of eyes were boring into Satan.

But a steady voice on the other side of the car froze them in their sockets.

"One move, you lousy bums, and you'll die of lead poisoning! Just button your lips while my 'lush' pal removes your hardware."

Satan's gun was in his hand as Slim started speaking. He jammed it into the ribs of the man on the side of the car, expertly frisked him for a hip gun, went into his coat for another cannon in an armpit holster. Slim had the other two covered, twin guns almost in their faces.

But Satan's man tried to break for it. The crew leader slammed him against the car, his hand on the gunman's throat. That skull cracked sickeningly twice, then a fast arcing smack with the muzzle of his .45 put him to sleep.

There were cars coming down the street. Satan lifted the fallen man by the collar, hurled him into the back of the car. "Duck your guns, Slim! I've got these two covered. Look out for the headlights of these cars!"

BUT AS far as appearances went, it was just a friendly group chatting by the curb that was revealed in the glare of lights from the oncoming cars. When the last of the cars were by, Satan jammed his gun hard into the ribs of the man nearest him, went over him quickly to bring his gun out. He dropped it into his pocket with the others he had brought to light, yanked out a set of 'cuffs and shackled the man's wrists behind his back. Then he pushed him onto the floor of the car.

Slim made fast work of the driver. He disarmed him, handcuffed him rapidly, thrust him into the back seat with the others. Satan made himself small in a corner. "Get down the road, Slim—about two miles," he snapped. "I'm going to have another singing session with these rats."

The crew lieutenant jumped in behind the wheel and started the car away at a fast clip. He swung into a side road, went on for maybe a mile, then came to a lane that led down into a ravine. Slim swung with the lane, found himself jolting down a steep hill. The lights of the car picked out the tall rubbish heap of a refuse dump. He swung around behind it, snapped the lights off.

"Get 'em out," Satan snapped to Slim. "This garbage dump is as good a place as any for these lads to end up!"

One of the men—the short, pinch-faced man who had been

The burly form of Arnleigh slammed across the desk.

driving—stood near Satan, his breath coming in gasps. "Whaddya mean, we end up on the garbage dump! Ain't youse guys bulls?"

"Of a sort," Satan told him grimly. "But not the sort that's best for your health—unless you talk! Who are you men? What are you doing up here? What was in that package you carried out of the car?"

No answer.

Satan dropped his gun and grabbed the man to him. "By God, I don't like to throttle a man when he's handcuffed! But I'll get the truth out of this one—or kill him!"

The savageness of the leader brought a whistle of amazement from Slim. The gaunt lieutenant watched Satan shake the man like a dog breaking a cat's back. He saw Satan smash the man hard, drop him, then jerk him erect and grip him by the throat.

"Do you talk?" Satan snarled. "Do you talk to me? Or do I kill you with my bare hands!" The crew leader grunted as he went to work on the man. The gunman croaked his terror, moaned wildly.

"Let up! F'r God's sake, let up! The fortune teller will throw the book at me, if the coppers get me—but—*ouch... oh!*" he gasped again as Satan went for him. "But anyway, the most I'll get will be life... not Death!"

Satan stood back, his eyes on the squirming figure. "You'll talk?"

"Yeah. *Yeah!* I'm talkin'."

"Shut up, Skimp," one of the other men called. "Raphael will cut your throat if you peep!"

"And I'll rip his throat out if he doesn't," Satan snarled. "Shut up, you rat!" He turned back to the little man. "You're one of Raphael's boys, eh? And the 'fortune teller,' the *judge,* will give you life? Is that what you mean by *throwing the book* at you?"

"Yeah," the man moaned. "I—I killed a bill-poster who tried to cross me up, in Michigan."

Satan snapped a look at his watch. "What are you doing up here?"

"We—we brung a bundle o' cotton, on orders."

"Cotton? You mean, counterfeit bills?"

"Yeah."

"Where is it?"

Silence.

Satan stepped forward. The little man moaned, tried to roll away. "It's in a tree, near the bank. All I had to do was hook the bundle o' cotton to a rope hangin' there, haul it up into the branches, an' fling the rope out o' sight, after it."

"You're a lying rat!"

"No! No I ain't."

"What was the idea of that? Who's it for?"

"I—I dunno. Raphael's got some new sort o' racket worked out for his cotton. Instead of ordinary bill-posting, this new game is such that he don't have to give no split to cotton wholesalers. But that's all I know, so help me!"

Satan considered the thing. Then he pulled Slim aside. "Do you get it? The usual counterfeiting game is run by a manufacturer, who makes the money, which is then sold to a wholesaler, at so much per hundred dollars of phony. The wholesaler has 'retail' men in the various cities who buy from him and pass the queer around. But in some way, Raphael has hooked into a game where he passes the money straight. But... *how?*"

"Through the banks," Slim stooged for him.

"Right! But, why should he *bother* to pass queer if he can *get at* the bank? Why put the bills out at all if he can get good dough from the source?" Satan asked!

Slim stirred in the dark, shrugged. "It's got me."

"Me, too." Satan looked at his watch again. "I've got to step on it, to get to that bank before closing time! Give me a hand and we'll tip this light car over!"

Slim lent a hand and the two men pushed at one side of the car... tilted it... sent it over on its side with a thud.

With the car on its side, Satan clambered up on it and pulled a rear door open. He didn't waste any time with niceties on the murderous trio. He jumped down, picked the men up one after another and threw them onto the skyward side of the car. Then he went up again, dumped them down into the car. He found a piece of cable in the dump heap, quickly lashed the handles of the car doors together. He came down again, found an old can nearby. He thrust the captured guns into the receptacle and hid the small arsenal of weapons under some refuse.

"Let's go," Satan snapped.

As they walked, he said to Slim: "I'm going to leave that bundle of queer where it is. I'm not even going to look for it. If I can get into that bank, I'll hide and watch what happens. It's a cinch that counterfeit money isn't going to stay there *overnight!* It would be seen in the morning.

Slim shook his head. "But, Captain! If the banker—Ezra

Timkens—is in on this thing, and we've got him, then how can we follow this thing through?"

"You mean, maybe he's supposed to get the dough and plant it in the bank?"

"Doesn't it look that way?"

"Well," Satan said, as they turned up the street for the bank again, "if Ezra Timkens is in on this... the president of the bank... then the bundle of queer will be there in the morning. And we're that much further along the trail! If it *does* disappear—then it must be going into the bank without Timkens knowing about it. But I'll be there, watching! Where is Timkens now?"

"Gentleman Dan and The Dutchman have him, in the car, on one of the back roads. They're to drive over near the coal yard—a couple of blocks from the bank—when the town has settled down for the night."

"Okay. I'm going into the bank now, to change a bill. If I can spot a hideout in there, I'll stick. If I can't, I'll hide in back of the place and see what happens. Stick close. Slim, in case I get jammed up! And handle that decoy act exactly as I told you!"

CHAPTER 11
OUT OF THIN AIR

B ANKER EZRA Timkens was tired, after his cold supper at home. He felt vaguely nervous as he arose from the table. "Because of the storm that's brewing," he mused, as he walked from the big table into his den. "Or maybe it's Ella and the children bein' away at the seashore. This damn' place is lonesome."

He dropped into a chair to read his evening paper for a few minutes before going back to the bank. These Saturday nights gave him a pain in his wrinkled and browned neck.

"Them new-fangled idees o' Belmann's," he muttered darkly. "O' course, it does bring in the business—but it ain't worth all the bother. Insurance departments… savin's departments… Christmas Clubs… new-fangled devices an' contraptions t' guard the bank. Heck!"

He was nosing into the sporting sheet of the paper when the doorbell rang. Old Maisie, the family cook and general factotum, grumbled as she went to the door. "A body can't get no dish-washin' done nowadays," she grumbled. She snapped the porch light on and peered through the screen door. "Yes? What is it?"

A tall, suave, dark young man made her a low bow. "Is Mr. Timkens at home?"

The hired woman wiped her hands on her apron and tried not to compare this young man with Clark Gable. She liked Gable in the movies, and hated to admit this man was better looking. But the fat, blond, pink-cheeked man who was with him didn't shock Old Maisie's romantic eyes, either.

"He might be, and then again he mightn't be," Old Maisie said. But Banker Timkens wasn't averse to a little company before he went back to the grind. He defeated Old Maisie's purpose.

"Who is it? Come in! What's the matter with you, Maisie? Is that any way to treat callers?"

"Not t' my way o' thinkin'," Old Maisie huffed at him, as she let the visitors in. "But it's the way you told me to do." She shuffled down the hall to the kitchen.

The tall, suave, dark man came alone... the other halting in the hall. "Mr. Timkens? I'm here on business about the bank." He flashed a badge quickly, then put it away again.

"Huh? Glory be, what's wrong now?"

The caller shrugged. "Maybe nothing." He looked around, saw a telephone. "But you'd better call the bank and tell them you can't get back to-night. I haven't time to explain—so please hurry."

Ezra Timkens got to his feet. "Say! Now what in tarnation are you—" He gulped, stared at the businesslike gun that was in the caller's hand. "Kidnapers!"

"Shut it," his cool visitor ordered him. "No harm is coming to you, Mr. Timkens. I promise you that. Now, step to that 'phone and make that call!"

Timkens knew a tough proposition when he saw one. He had been one himself, most of his life. He decided to temporize with this man... whoever he was. He got up, went to the telephone, put in the call.

"'Lo, this you Jake?" He jumped when the muzzle of the gun bit into his back. "Look, Jake. I ain't a-comin' back to-night. No.... Jest lock up tight, as usual. I'll see ye Monday... I hope." He put the telephone down.

"Outside now," his captor told him tersely. "Then, call in to your hired woman and tell her not to wait up for you. Say you've been called to New York."

Timkens hesitated; then gave in. Old Maisie came into the hall, her mouth wide and her eyes round.

"Don't that beat all, the way men carry on when their family is away!" the woman grumbled. "Th' old stay-out!"

Memories of reading of countless other 'rides' drifted through Ezra Timkens' brain as the car he was thrust into rolled swiftly down the street....

SATAN WALKED into the bank and up to the teller's window. His eyes were busily sizing up the place. Few people were left, and the clerks were shutting up for the week-end. An overalled man was mopping the floors. The evening's business was nearly over.

Down a narrow hall that was screened from the street by a shade, was a door marked *Ezra Timkens, President.* Satan went to the teller's window on that side and took out a bill. "Can you change this for me, please?"

The man looked at Satan, saw nothing familiar in that clean-cut, rugged face or in those level, gray eyes that peered through bone-rimmed spectacles. He dropped his eyes to the bill.

"How do you want it?"

"Any way at all."

Satan watched the crisp, clean, genuine bills slither through the man's nimble fingers. He was pocketing them when some-one came in the door and shouted, "Hello, folks! Is it too late to get a drink in this joint?"

All eyes went to the tall, gaunt, sad-eyed but obviously tipsy man who was standing in the doorway. One of the tellers called: "This ain't a saloon, Mister. This is a *bank.*"

There was a general laugh from them all, and the eyes of the employees stayed riveted on the doleful-looking man as he negotiated the door after several false starts. Satan backed away from the window slowly, ducked when he reached the hallway.

The dark door of the president's office opened quickly and shut on him noiselessly.

The teller at the window where Satan had changed the bill turned, his eyes glinting. "It beats all how some people can git so hopped up," he said. "Is your change all right, Mister?"

He blinked suddenly, stared at the emptiness in front of him. "Must 'a gone out when I was watching that drunk," he murmured. He turned away, his tired eyes seeking the clock. "Heck! It's after closing time already. Hey, Jake! How about it?"

They made rapid work of trundling the cash to the vaults and slamming the big doors shut. "Ain't no one goin' to get *that* cash," the man called Jake observed with satisfaction. He snapped a light switch, dimming all the bulbs but one which glowed in front of the vault.

"What you suppose ol' Ezra is up to, heh?" he asked his companion, as they walked to the door. "The ol' fox! Beats all how a man his age will act up when his wife's away. Oh, well!"

The front door slammed shut and silence settled over the bank.

SATAN SAT quietly in the comfortable chair of Ezra Timkens' office as the hours ticked off on his wrist watch. The rumble of trains along the nearby tracks became less frequent. The home-going movie crowds filled the streets for a few moments, then they were gone.

It was close to midnight when the rain started to fall, a swift patter of heavy drops at first, then a steady downpour. Satan waited for another lengthy period, then rose and went slowly into the interior of the bank. The dim light that shone on the vault doors traced the shadowy aisle out to the front of the bank.

Satan crouched low and went swiftly to a side window, peered cautiously through the curtains. The street lights threw a golden glow on the rain-slick pavements; but there was no sign of life on that side street. Satan remembered the meeting place at the coal yard, down the street from the bank. He crouched again to make his way to that side and look out.

But there was nothing other than the swish of rain and the faint glow of the street lamps.

Satan went back toward the president's office. He halted suddenly at a loud rumble. A train was going by along the tracks; a train that was long, heavy, vibrating in Satan's ear drums. He peered out the curtained window, saw the slicked, white oblongs that rolled in a steady parade past the station, New York bound.

"The early milk train," Satan recognized it.

He stood away from the window, went into the dark hall that led to the president's office. But again he stopped, his muscles stiffening. From somewhere to the rear came a sound, a definite sound... scraping... and then a slight *thump.*

The crew leader swung silently, went out into the obscure interior. For a moment, he thought someone was trying that door. But he realized instantly that he was wrong. With the alarm system functioning, and in the light cast by the street lamp, it would have been worse than foolhardy. And Satan knew that the cunning but warped brain that was behind this systematic, under-cover bank smashing was anything but foolhardy.

He stood in the shadow of that far corner, the glass counter with its pens and ink and blotters at his elbow. There was the sound of a step from across the interior of the bank. Satan froze back into the corner further, crouched down slightly. His hand slid into his jacket and came out with his .45.

Two men were standing in the aisle that was opposite Satan, their eyes cocked in the direction of the big vault doors.

They were standing exactly where Satan had been but five minutes before, as if they had materialized out of the thin, still air of the bank.

CHAPTER 12
GHOST BANK

IT FLASHED through Satan's mind that these two wraiths had entered the bank in the same manner as he himself had entered it: before closing hours. But he remembered his tour of inspection of the place, remembered that there was no place where those men could have secreted themselves other than where Satan had sat in wait—in the office of President Ezra Timkens.

He stood without breathing for a moment, his eyes keened. One of the men stirred. Satan dropped low, crept silently under the glass ledge on which the customers made out their checks or deposit slips. There were light footfalls, then silence again.

The light seemed dimmed for a brief minute, and something dark seemed to reach for the ceiling of the bank, near the vault.

Satan crouched lower, but his eyes were trained on the safety vault. The light glowed as before... and the huge vault doors that stretched to the ceiling were looming behind it assuringly. Satan frowned when a metallic *spang* came to his ears. He heard whispers, shuffling steps. There was a slight creak, as of a heavy door swinging open on old, dried hinges.

Satan frowned and stood to see if the men were working with a trap door, inside the cages and near the vault. The sounds continued, but there was nothing to be seen. Satan came out of his corner slightly and craned his neck. The faintest shimmer of light seemed to come from the side of the vault.

The crew leader twisted his head, saw that the light would be invisible from the doorway or the front windows. The shade was down on the only window that might have commanded a view of the spot. He went forward and suddenly clamped his jaws hard against the gasp that rose to his lips.

He couldn't believe his eyes. He looked away a moment, then back again. But they were still there... those two figures... and behind the vault was *another* vault!—another vault whose doors were opened wide and within which two cool, hard-faced men were working swiftly and silently.

Satan realized the stunning truth, and his eyes ranged over the contraption that had grown suddenly in front of and almost completely around the vault whose doors stood wide. It was a screen! A black, polished screen that had been carried in, in some fashion, and snapped up in front of the real vault. Anyone passing outside—the policeman on the beat, a casual passerby, or even a man who worked daily in that bank himself—wouldn't have any inkling that cracksmen were working in that bank.

Satan wondered how they had opened the safe without an alarm sounding. But he pushed the puzzle into the background of his brain as he crouched where he could watch what was going on. Two more men suddenly materialized from nowhere and joined the two already working on the vault. Satan watched, fascinated, as the newcomers opened two small handbags and slipped rubber gloves on their hands.

ONE OF the new men—hard-faced, red-haired, narrow-eyed, took charge of the proceedings. He worked like a master surgeon, ordering the tools of his trade in a crisp, low voice, moving without hesitation or doubt, getting instant obedience from his men.

Bundle after bundle of bills he brought from the vault, passed them to the others, then re-entered the great safe to bring out more bills. As he passed them for packing, one man was keeping a tally.

"…Eighty!" he sang out, after a while. Then: "Ninety… one hundred grand!…" And, finally, "One hundred and ten thousand."

"Close it up," the red-haired one snapped.

"Closed!" the checker answered.

"Finger gloves," the voice said crisply. Satan frowned, wondering what was coming now. He saw the man with one satchel pass something wrapped in shiny paper. There was a crisp crackle, and the gloves were pulled on swiftly by the red-head.

"My God," Satan breathed. "They even wrap their things in cellophane!"

"Cotton!" the red-head's voice crackled.

"Cotton coming!"

Now, bills in neat bundles started to go back *into* the safe. A third man stood between passer and receiver and peered at each marking on the packages as bills started *back* into the safe. "Twenty-five," he called. "Forty… Forty-five… *Fifty*-five!"

The operation ceased momentarily. "Water!" the chief operator snapped. A bottle was passed into his hands and he sprinkled some liquid onto his gloves. Satan saw him step carefully into the vault, pick up bundle after bundle of the bills, and put them all down again. Then the leader of the eerie crew picked up and put down package after package of securities.

At length, he was through in the vault. But he didn't take his gloves off yet, "Shoes," he called.

"Shoes coming."

He took some sole-shaped things that were passed him and fitted them on his own shoes… like light over-shoes. "Water!" He passed some fluid over his feet, trod around the vault door heavily. Then:

"Letter."

A flat piece of paper was passed him. He took it gingerly between his fingers, then crouched low and made his way across the interior of the bank, through the gate to the aisle where Satan crouched, then along the darkened hall leading to the door of the president's office.

For a moment, Satan was tempted to sneak after the man,

to bat him over in silence and in darkness, and to come out and take the rest of the gang by surprise. But he checked the impulse.

"This isn't Krantz," he knew. "Nor Raphael. Krantz has dark hair, and Raphael is a muddy blond. I've got to get the man *behind* this mob."

In a moment, the red-headed leader was back, walking in a swift but ungainly crouch. He snapped off the vault lights, then closed the doors of the place. Carefully, he stood and pressed his gloved hands on the door, twirled the combination, then backed slowly off to the other side of the room, away from the safe.

"Mop!" he said crisply.

One of his assistants stepped forward and yanked a short mop from his pocket. He leaned forward, spilling water from a bottle and mopping up rapidly in front of the safe. The whole thing flashed into clear understanding in Satan's mind.

"A hundred and ten thousand taken out, and fifty-five thousand of 'cotton'—counterfeit—put back *in!* Half the amount!" His eyes shifted for a moment to the dark hall where the red-haired leader had disappeared, into Timkens' office. "And if that wasn't one of those extortion notes calling for the other half—calling for fifty-five thousand dollars—then I'm guessing a mile off!"

He watched the mopping work, fascinated. Two men had retreated, with the mopper going backward slowly, his small mop wiping up the footprints that had been made. The red-head waited, then stepped deliberately for the vault, reversed himself, stooped a moment behind the false-front that was a duplicate of the large safe.

He bent a spring rod; and the whole of the false front collapsed. It was rolled into a folding packet, the spring rods doubling over to fold the thing in a tight roll. Satan made his way to where he could crouch at the side of the marble counter and cover the front door. He heard a *thump* from the other side… then another. And quiet.

Voices came faintly from the rear of the bank, then died. The hum of a motor sounded. Satan frowned, then crept forward and peered around the edge of the counter. There was no sound. Outside, a motor riffed loudly and lights flashed along the street in front of the bank.

A feeling of unbelief and panic gripped Satan. Recklessly, he stood and ran around into the other aisle, his gun at ready. Only emptiness and the steady patter of rain greeted him. The wall and windows and counter were smooth and bare.

But men, bags and money were gone… vanished from the ghostly bank as if by magic. It had him stopped beautifully.

SATAN STOOD transfixed for a moment; then leaped for the front door of the place. He grabbed the safety catch and yanked the knob. The door came open when he turned a second catch, under the knob.

Instantly, the shrill scream of a siren split the air, and an alarm bell started clanging. Several blocks down, a car slammed into second speed and whined away into the dark… lightless.

The deafening uproar continued as Satan slammed the door behind him. He raced a few yards, tugging at a whistle. Shrill blasts of the police-type signal joined the clamor. A block down, by the coal yard, a motor roared alive and a car shot into the street, then stopped with a squealing of brakes.

Windows across the street were opening and hoarse shouts coming from the startled citizens of Tayloe City. Satan pounded along on his well-muscled legs and slid to a stop at the car. Slim was leaning out of the rear door, his mask on. Satan slammed into the tonneau and pulled the door shut.

"Follow the car that just went down the road," he shouted. Kayo jumped the long, swift limousine into a quick start and wheeled down the street. The scream of a police car's siren sounded far off across the tracks.

Satan snapped his mask out and donned it. He tried to sit down, but found the rear seat already crowded. He peered, holding onto Slim. He saw The Dutchman in one corner—Slim was in the other. But the man in the middle was a stranger. Satan stared. "Who's this?" he asked. "Ezra Timkens?"

Slim said, "Right, Captain. He's been pretty decent, too. But he's certain we're a band of cut-throats and kidnapers."

"Kee-rect!" the indignant banker snapped. "I'd have had th' Law onto ye only these murderers 'a been sittin' with guns in m' ribs!"

Satan didn't answer him. "Gentleman Dan and Kayo up front?"

"Yes, Captain," Slim answered quickly.

"Good. I couldn't have a better gang of scrappers for the job we have on. Did you see those fellows go into the bank?"

Slim sat up. "Huh? Into the Bank of Tayloe?"

"Yes. Four men. They hit the vaults and are slamming for

home with one hundred and ten thousand dollars in their bags! Half that much—fifty-five thousand—is in the Tayloe Bank's vaults... *in cotton!*"

"Be ye crazy?" Timkens shrilled. "How in tarnation could a body get that much cotton into my vaults, let alone my bank? Ye're a bunch of murderin' lunatics, if y'ask me."

"And if *you* ask *me,*" Satan grinned, "you'd better lie right down on the floor of this car if we catch up with those hoods. That's one very tough, experienced, cool mob of yeggs that we're chasing!"

Timkens blinked, but Satan had turned away, was rolling down the window between the driver and the rear compartment. "Slim! Get out the artillery. You, Kayo! Give it all you can. We've *got* to get that gang!"

Kayo hunched his big shoulders harder over the wheels. The car was hitting eighty over the slicked road, but he trod even harder on the accelerator, now.

"You know me, Cap'n!"

"I don't think those lads will try any tricks," Satan said. "They won't make any fancy turn-offs—not for a while, yet. They figure they've got the fastest car in the county, and they'll probably highball straight along for twenty miles or so."

Slim twisted in his seat. "Headlights coming along behind us," he said. After a pause, he added, "They're not gaining, though."

"Coppers," Satan grunted. "I hope they haven't started any teletype messages going."

Up front, Kayo grunted. "Something sliding along about a mile ahead, Cap'n! See it? Close in to the trees?"

Gentleman Dan said, "What an imagination! How can you see anything a mile off in this rain?" But he took the tommy-gun that Slim passed to him and slapped the three hundred-round drums on the seat at his side.

"Say! Who are you men, anyway?" Timkens asked, his voice puzzled. "You ain't cops. You ain't Federal men. Be ye a rival gang?"

"We're *private* cops," Satan said. "And you'd better pray that we catch those yeggs and beat 'em; or your bank and your reputation will be blown into the mountains!"

A sudden chatter of machine-gun fire raised above the purr of the wheels and the high-pitched hum of the motor. Kayo cranked a small wheel near his left hand, and a metal arm crept some ten feet out from the car. He snapped a switch and a powerful searchlight came alive from the end of that arm, speared through the rain and the dark to light up the rear of another limousine.

The firing from that other car centered on the searchlight, smacked hard on the steel arm, splintered the powerful lens in a thousand bits of flying glass. But the decoy-light had served its purpose. Gentleman Dan was lying partly out of the window of the speeding car, and he trained his tommy-gun on the orange jets that spurted from the car ahead.

For a full drum he held it, hosing the back of the car, the gas tank and the wheels. A white warning sign flashed by—there was an intersection ahead. The bandit car was skidding wildly from side to side, slowing perceptibly. Gentleman Dan snapped

111

another drum into place while Satan opened fire, through the rear window... firing parallel with the car's side.

The Dutchman was holding his gun in readiness at the other window. Gentleman Dan had loaded again, was thrusting his gun through the port in the windshield to open another blast when the gunner's car shot along sideways for a hundred feet, then negotiated the cross-road ahead, swiping several yards of white fencing as it went.

Kayo stood on his clutch, slammed on his brakes, and spun the wheel. The heavy, underslung limousine pivoted like a top, spun madly one... two... three... four turns, in the intersection. As it slowed its whirling, Kayo flipped into second gear and jerked the car out of the spin.

He ripped into the fence, was through it, bounced madly across a shallow ditch, righted the careening vehicle, and stood on the gas pedal again. His headlights jumped alive for the first time, picked out the car ahead. The Dutchman, Gentleman Dan and Satan opened fire simultaneously.

The bank cracker's limousine heeled wildly, straightened suddenly, then slowed. A hail of lead smacked against the front windshield of the crew car, covering it with a frosted surface. Kayo cursed low and steadily as he ducked still lower. He slammed the brakes on suddenly, flipped the wheel of the car to the left.

The outlaw car had tried to limp along on two bullet-torn tires, had come to grief in the ditch on the right side of the road. Satan leaned far out of his window and smashed a withering burst of fire into the car. A figure detached from the crumpled vehicle and sprinted for the near woods…

…A figure that carried a handbag.

Slim stuck his automatic close to Satan's ear and squeezed the trigger gently, pumped six shots at the fleeing gangster. The man staggered, came to his knees, tried to get up again. Slim squeezed once more and the man flopped crazily.

SATAN WAS out of the car, his tommy-gun at ready. "Hold it," he called to the others. "There may be some trouble still, in that carload." He raised his voice: "You've got five seconds to come out of there, with your hands up!"

A burst of firing came from the back of the car, slapped harshly on the armored crew car near where Satan stood. The leader fired back into that blaze of flame, holding his tommy-gun at his hip. When he stopped, there was utter silence… only the ticking of something in the wrecked car, and the patter of rain.

"Turn two guns on that wreck before you go into it," Satan called. "Watch out that you don't spray me!" He sprinted across the ditch and into the field. Gentleman Dan went after him, as another chatter of gunfire raised on the air.

Satan flashed his light on the man in the field, stopped it on that handbag. He came close, opened it. It was the bag with the money, the bag with the hundred and ten thousand dollars. He picked it up, turned to see Gentleman Dan stooping over the limp form of the gunman. The crewman's own flash was on the gruesome bundle of torn flesh and clothes, was picking out the red hair that was strangely askew on that blasted head.

"Teddy Krantz!" Gentleman Dan said softly. "By God, we got him! The rat! He killed two pals of mine, while I was still working for the Secret Service!"

"What?" Satan asked. "That isn't Krantz! That man has bright red hair. Krantz's head is black as a crow's."

Gentleman Dan reached out a hand and tugged at that red hair. It came away from a closely-cropped, dark skull.

"Print him," Satan snapped. "I want the prints of this entire mob."

"What'll I use?" Gentleman Dan asked.

Satan shook his head slowly. "Use anything, Dan—for paper. But I think there's enough blood spilled here to wet his fingers with." He went back to the car, carrying the bag. Slim met him.

"All dead," he said.

"I imagined so," Satan said slowly. "Print them all, Slim. Get that other bag they were carrying, the bag with the equipment. Search the men and strip them of all guns and papers. I'm going to make life hell for whoever passed those tommy-guns on to them... after I trace them back."

"Right, Captain." Slim gestured with his head. "That other mug dead?"

Satan nodded. "Yes, Slim. Teddy Krantz is dead." The crew leader walked over to his own car, looked in at the dazed banker who sat there under guard of The Dutchman.

"Well, I got your money."

Timkens came out of it, snorted his defiance. "A fat lot o' good that'll do *me!* Looks like I'm out, no matter who gets the money."

Satan's eyes were earnest behind his mask. "Will it convince you if I give you your money, drive you back to your bank, show you just what went on there? Will it?"

Timkens blinked. "You mean—you ain't agoin' t' take that money? An' me, too?"

Slim was coming up with the results of his search. A small arsenal of guns... another bag... a wad of personal papers. From nearby, a siren rose into the night air. Satan barked an order.

"Hop in, all! The cops have picked up the trail. Douse your lights, Kayo, and go straight down this road. We will argue this thing as we go."

TWENTY MINUTES later, Ezra Timkens stirred in his seat. "Mebbe I'm crazy as a loon," he said, "an' no wonder! Sech a night as I put in to-night will turn my hair gray! But—"

Satan sensed the man's hesitation, saw that his argument was all but won. "What color do you think your hair is now," he grinned. "Pink?"

"Eh? Who has pink hair? Don't get fresh with me, feller, just because ye've got guns and masks!"

"Well, how about it?" Satan asked again. "Near Tayloe City I'll drop my men and just two of us—unmasked—will go to your bank with you. I want to show you what has been happening to you... and to those other banks that have been robbed, and those bank presidents who have died... the 'suicides.' "

Timkens shuddered. "It don't sound true," he whispered. "My God, what would Ellie and the children think if—" He broke off, a scheming gleam in his eyes. "Will ye let me hold th' money?"

"You can hold it," Satan said. "It isn't mine. I make no claim to it."

The banker cheered visibly. "An' one o' them tommy-guns, too?"

"Not on your life! Well, is it a deal? Do you appoint me a private investigator, and keep shut to the police and anyone else?" But he shook his head. "Damned if I think you can get into that bank tonight, or over Sunday. You'll have to wait for the alarm system to be fixed."

Timkens bristled. "I guess I c'n git into my own bank if I want to!" He barked at Kayo, "Drive on! What are ye waitin' fer?"

Satan grinned. "After, all, it doesn't seem to be such a stunt to get into *your* bank, Mr. Timkens!"

CHAPTER 13
THE CHINK USES HIS HEAD

EZRA TIMKENS sat at his desk, counting the money he had taken from the handbag. He tallied each packet in neat figures. When he was through, he totaled the sum.

"One hundred and ten thousand dollars," he said softly. "But—I won't believe this came out o' my vaults until I see f'r myself."

"Open them up," Satan shrugged. Slim watched the man curiously, stirred at the blush that came over his features.

"I can't," the banker confessed. "Thet danged time lock is on, an' I can't move it."

Satan blinked. "Krantz opened it," he said. He thought for a moment, then said, "Well? You trust us enough by now? Pull down *all* the shades. I want to bring one of my men in to look your wiring system over. It's a policy of mine not to let my men see me any more clearly than I can help. I want to re-mask. And I want Slim re-masked, too."

A daring look came into Timkens' eyes. "Let's blow the danged thing open!"

"Say," Satan said. "What's got into you, anyway? Damned if I don't think you have the makings of a cracksman in you, at that!" He turned to Slim. "Get The Chink. Tell him to lug his stuff in here—all of it."

While the lieutenant was gone, a violent hammering shook the front door. Timkens crossed and opened it. Three uniformed policemen were standing there, "What's going on in here?" one of them asked. "Your alarm went off some time ago, an' there was an awful racket." He paused for breath. "'Sides, a gangster car wuz wrecked down to Clayham township, an' there's all hell to pay. Four men dead."

"You're tellin' me," Timkens said.

"What?" The policeman stared. Satan moved nervously. But the banker corrected himself. "I mean, you don't tell me. But listen, fellers—me an' my private detective is goin' over important matters, an' we don't want to be bothered any more. G'night."

He slammed the door.

Slim was back in ten minutes with The Chink. Both men were masked. Satan slid his own silk cloth over his face as the two men came in. The crew leader explained matters slowly, The Chink nodding his understanding. When he had finished, The Chink went over and examined the vault curiously.

"The bank has two systems, yes?" he addressed Timkens. "One from the power house—one private, in case the power goes off?"

"Yeah," Timkens growled. "That's Belmann's idee. It costs a lot of money, but it's good."

The Chink grinned. "The system is good, eh? Yet a man can get in!" He went off to trace the wiring system of the bank. Satan took Timkens across the polished floor, stopped near the vault.

Lead hammered against the windshield.

There were footmarks with a peculiar rounded splotch in the center of each.

"See those?" Satan asked. He opened the equipment bag that the Brantz mob had toted, fished out a pair of fashioned soles that could slip on like overshoes.

119

"Just like my shoes," the banker exclaimed. "I wear little rubber circles to keep me from slippin' on these floors."

"Just like yours is correct," Satan said grimly. "Could you have proved you weren't here last to-night—if it had been put to you? Those are your footprints! Made from a sample of your shoes!"

Timkens gasped, but Satan was pointing to the vault door. "See those fingerprints there?" He stooped, pulled out a set of rubber gloves with the fingers of them whorled and circled like a human's fingers.

"See these gloves? See the fashioned finger tips on them? See how they are all over that vault door? There are more marks inside... on securities... on packets of bank notes... on the walls."

"What of it?"

Satan smiled, lifted the man's hand, stared at it. He fetched a stamp pad, inked one of Timkens' fingers and pressed it down on a piece of paper. He did the same with the corresponding finger of the glove. "Identical prints," Satan said. "Not exact, maybe, but close enough for the police to identify them as yours. Could you have laughed *that* off if money was missing from your vaults on Monday morning?"

"Gosh ding!"

"Follow me." Satan went back into the office of the president, went through the desk drawers rapidly. He found some personal papers, pulled them out. Among them was a straight, unfolded note that was typewritten and bore Saturday's date. The note ran:

Ezra Timkens,

If you value the life of your wife and the safety of your children, you will be at your bank Saturday night after closing to give my messenger fifty-five thousand dollars.

It was unsigned.

"Ever see that before. Timkens?"

"No," the man gasped.

Satan peered at it. "Hm. Well, it's got your prints on it. The note hasn't been folded, so it wasn't mailed. And I'll tell you another thing, too. This type matches some typewriter in this bank... a typewriter that you use, or could have used." He passed the letter to Slim. "See if you can find that typewriter, Slim. There are some over there by the secretary's desk."

Timkens dropped into his chair, his face frightened. "But," he said weakly, "I could'a proved I didn't do it"

"You think so? Saugers didn't have a chance to prove it. Cossart didn't have a chance to prove it. Here's something else, too. On Monday morning, your tellers would have taken that cotton—that counterfeit money—and started cashing checks and making change with it."

"Why?"

Satan shook his head. "That's what I'd been wondering. I think I have the answer, now. This gang has linked bank robbery and counterfeiting. The thing was done this way: the gang, in some way, got in and out of your bank. How, I don't know yet. They'd take a large sum of money and replace *half that sum* with counterfeit bills. In that way, the money shortage would be such that you could conceivably have taken it. Why? Because *half* the sum was in counterfeit, back in the vault, and that additional loss would go undetected for some days. By that time, Mr. Timkens—*you* would be dead… dead in jail. The bonding company would pay, and there you are."

"But, why'n heck didn't they take it *all?* All the money that was in the vault?"

"That would spoil the game. Then the police would *know* that there was a rat somewhere. You see, this gang plans to do a big business with a *number* of banks. Result? Terror… suspicion… panic, maybe. And while the police are running in circles, the gang mops up and steps out of the picture again, until they'd hit on some *new* wrinkle!"

The blood had drained from Timkens' face. The Chink rapped at the door and came in. He announced simply, "We can open the safe."

SATAN, SLIM and Timkens watched the little Oriental as he stood under the compact alarm boxes on the vault walls.

"That," The Chink said, pointing to one, "is the power system. This other is the independent system. What happens if the power goes off?"

Timkens blinked. "You mean, would an alarm ring?"

"Exactly."

The banker shook his head. "That would be a damned nuisance. No; it wouldn't ring. If the outside power is turned off, the inside system is automatically hooked in."

The Chink nodded. "Right. Now I'll break the outside system by ripping a wire." The Chink climbed onto a chair and jerked a wire loose from the box. "Now the inside system works. If I touch the vault, the alarm system works, right?"

"Yes," Timkens nodded. "So what?"

"So," The Chink demonstrated further, "I'll rip the inside system wire loose now—and you can open the safe."

Timkens gasped. "But it's a *time* alarm! It can't open until the clock reaches a certain hour."

The Chink shook his head, a smile splitting his masked features. "Did you ever *try* to open it after you set the time system? *This* time system?"

"Why, no. But look here, man! What the hell do you mean? How on earth could the manufacturer of this time device excuse that?"

"Accidents will happen," The Chink said simply. "Try the vault, please."

Timkens looked at him for a moment, then shrugged his shoulders.

The banker stepped forward, twirled the dials, yanked the handle. There was a metallic *clank* and a squeaking of the hinges as the doors swung. Satan stared at the time apparatus, listened to the tick of it, then turned to The Chink.

"How did you know that, Chink? I don't see anything wrong!"

The Chink shrugged. "I asked myself, 'Which is better? To believe Cap'n Satan when he sees the door open? Or to believe the time clock?' One is a liar, yes?" The Oriental smiled broadly. "I thought it safer to call the time clock a liar!"

Timkens was in the vault, staring at the neatly stacked money, was on his knees examining it. "By God, some of it *is* counterfeit," he roared. "But it's almost perfect!"

"Done by an artist," Satan said. "Masterpieces by Raphael!"

He pointed out the fingerprints on the securities, on the bills, on the inside walls. "Do you still think you could have talked your way out of *that?*"

Timkens' face was sober, his eyes wide. "No," he said. "No, I couldn't. You're right… Satan! They had me!"

"Yes. But I haven't got *them* yet." Satan turned to The Chink, described how the men had appeared, then disappeared, miraculously. "Not a door or a window open," he said. "No alarm rang until *I* opened the door when I realized they were making a getaway."

The Chink stared at the walls of the place. "Mr. Timkens, please… the system here is puzzling. The walls are made with the signal wire inside, so that each stone in the building is part of the alarm system, aren't they? Each stone makes a connection with the next stone, so it cannot be chopped through. Isn't that right?"

Satan cut in. "What do you mean, Chink? I don't get that."

"The stones are reïnforced with metal inside, yes?" At Satan's nod, he went on, "The alarm system wires up *all* the metal in the stones into one link. If *any* stone is damaged, any wire broken, any window or door moved while the alarm is on, the siren and bells sound."

Satan examined the floor for a trap door, but there was none. He shook his head, moved around in the aisle. Suddenly he snapped out his flash, trained the glowing ray on the floor, followed it to the wall under the glass counter on that side. There were faint mop marks visible.

"Now, what the devil!" Satan stood erect, stared at The Chink for a moment, then he squatted again. He found and picked up a small white shred of damp cotton. "This is from that *small* mop," he said. "They were mopping over this way to erase their own tracks. So if they went this way—" He stared at the blank, solid wall—peered at the whitish, rock-like filling between the large, white stones of the building.

His eyes were blazing when he turned to The Chink. "You have a metal testing device? An instrument that can locate metal... where there is any?"

The Chink nodded. "Radio-magnet machine. A small model of same thing which the men at Alcatraz call the Mechanical Eye. It detects metal—guns, knives, collar-buttons, even." He went into the front of the bank and dragged back a solid box with two small glass bulbs in the top. He found a base plug for a stand lamp, pulled the light wire loose and plugged his machine in.

"Now what?" he asked.

"Try these stones," Satan said simply. The Chink's face spread into a grin under his mask. He pointed the snout of the machine at a stone, from a few feet away. "It shows metal," he said. "The stones all have metal wiring."

Satan came over, impatience in his manner. "Shove it closer! Shove it right against the stones! The way you're doing it, the wiring in any of the stones would affect the machine."

The Chink moved the instrument almost against the wall. The red bulb in the top of the box shone brightly. "When there is no metal, the white light shows," The Chink explained. "Metal draws magnets and makes for the red light. When there is no metal—" He stopped, his mouth dropping in surprise.

125

"When there's no metal, a white light shows," Satan snapped. "And the white light is showing now! On that bottom stone. Try the one next it."

A red light showed.

"Try the one above it!"

The white light flashed on again and Satan sighed. Despite the fact that daylight was breaking over the village and that he was still masked, the crew leader made a quick measurement from the window to the stones which the instrument had shown to hold no wiring. Then he went rapidly out into the open.

He made his way to the side of the bank, measured from the window, as he had done inside, then down from the level of the window. He picked at one of the stones with his fingernail, then snapped a pocketknife open and dug it into the hard filling between two stones.

The stuff crumbled and rapidly, Satan hacked the filling loose from the two vertically placed stones. He thrust his fingers into the small opening and jerked. The entire outside piece came off in his hand. It was a flat, square-shaped piece like the others; but instead of a solid, granitelike mass weighing hundreds of pounds, it was only a thin imitation.

Inside was some padding of some sort. Satan pulled it out quickly. "Sound deadening material," he muttered. "That's how this false side was blocked against noise giving it away, or cold seeping through!"

He yanked the flat piece from the section vertically above, and then another from atop it. He scooped out the padding, made an opening large enough to crawl through. He trained his flash on the slabs that faced into the bank, saw two leather grips on them. The grips had probably been set in when the pieces were poured. He gripped one, pushed with his fist... and he nearly sprawled headlong into the bank. Then he pushed the other one out and crawled through to confront the astounded Slim, The Chink and the dazed banker.

"There's your answer," Satan said, standing up.

"But," Slim protested, "wouldn't the filling show lighter on those stones in the daylight? Couldn't it be seen, when it was replaced?"

Satan shook his head. "The rain, Slim. The rain evened it all up. These fellows evidently carried some sort of plastering putty that hardened quickly, dried out the same color as the other stuff. Especially with water to slick it down for a day or so.

"But," Slim gasped, "do you mean that this is how they get into *all* the banks?"

"All the *new* banks, Slim—of the Intra-State group! They're planned this way, these banks. And built this way. Probably the gang slips a foreman in on the job to handle this ticklish business, but—" He turned to Timkens. "Where did these stones come from?"

The banker shrugged. "Some place in New Jersey, I think. They put in a remarkably low bid for the material, so I gave them the order. I put it through Belmann, of course—of the Intra-State Association."

Satan stood silent for a long time. When he stirred, his voice was dry. "Someone has slipped one over on Belmann," he said. "I'll be the first to tell him—on Monday morning. Meanwhile,

Mr. Timkens, I want you to say absolutely nothing about this. I got Krantz. And now I'm after Raphael. Getting one without

the other is just like killing one bedbug and letting others stay alive to nest again."

Satan's first two slugs caught Gartano in the neck.

"But, the counterfeit money? And the hole in the wall of my bank!"

"Hide the money. Place a night and day guard at this spot, when you put those fake stones together again," Satan told him. "But I can't impress you too much on this one point. *Not a word to anyone;* not even to Belmann, if you should be talking with him. I want to find out where that plant is—the plant that builds phony stones and phony wiring systems for banks!"

Slim said, "What about the other new banks of the group? They're probably all set out in a line for a killing."

"Krantz's death will stop them for a day or two. When and if we get Garfano, then we can spread the word to the others. If we fail... if Raphael Garfano gets us—?" Satan shrugged. "Then Mr. Timkens is delegated to carry on for us."

"It's dangerous," Timkens protested.

"Look," Satan said. "I'm doing all right up to now. Why not let me finish the job? Besides—" he smiled slightly, "I'm not in this business for my health. This work takes money... and I'm out to take Garfano and Krantz for every penny that can't be claimed by anyone else!"

"I see." Timkens looked disappointed. "I'd get a kick out of telling this to Belmann, though. He's always so... so uppish and know-it-all."

"No," Satan ruled. "Someone's slipped it over on Belmann, and *I'm* the one to tell him. Will you shake on that, Mr. Timkens?"

"I'll shake," the man said, sticking out his hand. "And while I'm shaking on that, I'll just say thanks for... saving my bank, my reputation and my life. And—" the old chap paused, grinned

130

slightly, "if you ever need a banker to help with your work, Captain Satan—I'm your man!"

Satan shook heartily. "I don't forget quickly, Mr. Timkens." He turned to Slim.

"Have that counterfeit gang over in the dump shipped to a police station. Send their prints, and the ones we got tonight, to the F.B.I. And to the Treasury Department, too. Tell the boys off for a rest, but I want them for special instructions at the warehouse tomorrow night—*this* night, I mean. Split the crew and get them home individually. But collect all arms and ammunition, first. That's all, Slim."

"Right, Captain."

Satan turned and was gone. Timkens shook his head, his eyes grave. "That's the toughest and the smartest police department in the land," he said.

Slim smiled. "That's a lot of praise, Mr. Timkens. The F.B.I. men and the Treasury agents are smart and tough, too. But Captain Satan isn't chasing crime by man-made laws. He doesn't stop at any state lines. Captain Satan goes where crime is—and smashes it!"

The Chink shook his head sadly. "The Cap'n is a fine man. Too bad he is not Chinese!"

CHAPTER 14
SATAN'S TRAP

EARLY MONDAY morning, Satan stood outside the office building of the Intra-State Associates' offices. In his polo coat, cap and bone glasses, he was a conspicuous figure. But he didn't seem to know this, as he stared at the columns of his morning newspaper. The article he was reading ran:

> Police are holding a mysterious man who was suspected of planning an attempt on the life of Tobias Ellert, embezzling banker of the bank of Midcity, New York.
>
> Following an anonymous tip, police followed the man to the cell where Ellert was sleeping. The man, who represented himself as a lawyer, was found to be carrying a powerful drug in lethal quantities. Police are investigating him.

Satan folded the paper over, shook his head when another article came to his attention.

> Treasury agents are tracing the source of some counterfeit bills of ten and twenty-dollar denomination which were passed in nearby upstate New York. The bills are of good design and workmanship, but on close comparison with genuine bills, it can be observed that they are of a brighter green.

A swank, dark limousine drew up to the curb and two men stepped down. Satan looked, saw Belmann and Arnleigh, turned into the doorway and stood with his back towards them. When the men passed him, Satan went outside again.

It was a clear, bright day. Overhead, an airplane was circling lazily over lower Manhattan. Satan craned his neck to stare at it, then looked at the car Belmann had come in. It was parked a few feet down the curb. He put his hand in his pocket and took out a square, flat package. He unwrapped it gingerly, looked at it closely. It was made of shiny tin and looked like a type of mirror popular in the Army.

Satan walked down the steps and approached the car. He put his hand on the roof of the automobile and leaned down to talk with the driver.

"Are you taking Mr. Belmann up-county to-day? You're his driver, aren't you?"

The stolid, bull-necked man in driver's uniform stared at Satan for a moment. "Why don't you ask him? He's upstairs?"

Satan laughed. "Okay, I guess I will. Nice car you have here."

The driver blinked and looked away. Satan lingered a moment more, then went into the building. He wiped his hands on his handkerchief, but his fingers stayed sticky. He went into an elevator and called for the Intra-State office floor.

When he walked down the hall, he was whistling merrily and there was a hard glint in his eyes. He rapped briefly on the door, then pushed it open and walked in. Belmann was standing in his private office, his eyes trained on the door as Satan came in. Pam Pollarde, Belmann's secretary, was sitting at her desk, her eyes wide.

"Morning," Satan called cheerfully. He grinned at the girl, then turned to Belmann. "Someone has slipped something over on you, Belmann. I wanted to tell you personally—because of our differences."

A voice behind Satan spoke sharply, rapping out six terse, hard words.

"Don't move, sucker... or you'll die!"

SATAN LOOKED into the mirror on Belmann's wall and

saw Arnleigh, his eyes raging and his hair awry, standing behind him, a sub-machine gun gripped tightly in his hands.

Arnleigh spoke again. "Smart guy 'Satan.' huh? Why, ya cheap punk, if Belmann hadn't held off ya, I'd have blasted a hole a foot wide through that thick skull of yours."

Satan stood immobile, his eyes tense. Belmann laughed softly. "Did you see the sucker way he tried to duck us, downstairs? And the way he barged through the door, just now? And this is Satan—the tough cop!"

Both men laughed. Pam Pollarde sobbed suddenly, drew a choking breath. "Shut up, you!" Arnleigh snarled. "You're a swell lookin' doll, but you'll look as messy as any of them if I turn this lead hose on you!"

Satan stirred. "Listen, Belmann. I came here to tell you that someone put one over on you. Krantz and three of his men pulled a boner up in Tayloe City, early Sunday morning. I tracked them and knocked them off. The works are shot. I've solved the mystery of the strange embezzlements."

Belmann's face darkened. "Imagine," he said to Arnleigh. "Imagine a punk as stupid as this one doing in Teddy Krantz, and smashing up the play we had set! Get a load of it!"

"Let's bump him," Arnleigh suggested, moving closer.

Belmann snapped, "Raphael has given orders to bring him direct to *him*. He's wild enough now, without your making things worse by disobeying him. Come on, Satan. Stick those hands up while I search you."

Belmann patted Satan's pockets, frowned, jerked his coat

open and felt around under the armpits and over his chest. "Well, I'll be damned. He hasn't even got a rod on him!"

"What'll we do with the moll?" Arnleigh asked, his eyes leering.

"Take her along, of course. We can't leave her here, can we?"

Arnleigh chuckled evilly. "That don't hurt me none, pal!" He turned to the girl. "Get your hat on, Toots. We're goin' places. An' if I hear one little squawk out of you, you'll never ruin another letter on your typewriter!"

Satan stirred. "Say, Belmann, I hope you know what you're doing."

Belmann laughed. "Do I? And I love it. I've heard a lot about you, Satan. You've put some pretty good friends of mine under the sod and others behind bars. I always imagined you were a tough cookie. But—" He shrugged. "Now, in the elevator, and in the automobile, we're going to have our hands in our pockets; and if you make one move, utter one sound, I'll let you have it just as sure as God made little apples."

Arnleigh motioned to Belmann to cover Satan. He yanked a heavy grip out from behind a desk and 'broke' the machine gun. He packed it expertly, threw in some drums of ammunition that he took from the small safe in the place, and snapped the thing shut.

"Everything else was packed yesterday," he said to Belmann. "I smelled a rat when I heard that radio flash about Krantz and the boys." He shook his head. "You took an awful chance in coming back here."

Belmann grinned. "In my coat closet," he said smoothly, "is a

135

little valise with fifty grand packed away in it." He chuckled at Arnleigh's expression. "As we have so ably demonstrated with the Intra-State banks, the best place to keep your nest egg is right out in the open." His chuckle broadened to laughter. "If you'd only known that, eh, Arnleigh?"

Satan cut in on them. "Belmann, I take it you're confessing to a part in these bank robberies and the floating of that cotton. Right?"

"Confessing?" Belmann said scornfully. "I'm *boasting* about it!" His voice went hard, suddenly. "Let's scram out of here. For all we know, this punk may have some pals coming down here to tip us off to the big, bad mens who are robbing banks. Step on it, Arnleigh. You— Pollarde—get into your bonnet. Quick!"

SATAN SAT between Arnleigh and Belmann, on the back seat, as the car wound across town and slid down into the Holland tunnel. Pam Pollarde was on one of the small seats, her face drawn and her teeth chattering. When they stopped at the police gate to the tunnel to pay their way, Satan stirred slightly. Instantly, two concealed guns leaped into his ribs. He sighed and sat back. In the tunnel, he said, "Well, Belmann, there's no harm in telling me now, is there? How did you frame this Intra-State Bankers racket? It's an old outfit, isn't it? Your office?"

Belmann laughed boastfully. "The name is old. I bought into it five years ago, stupid. Five years of careful planning... five years or arguing with bankers, of framing schemes, of selling myself to those old crackpots who headed the banks. And then I started to cash in—" his voice took on an edge, "until you came along!"

Satan shook his head sadly. "Belmann, it's too bad you dumb

crooks never wise up to yourselves." When Belmann started savagely to speak, he said, "Oh, I don't mean you're thick—like your pal Arnleigh, here. But any crook is dumb. He's dumb thinking he is getting away with it. He's twice as dumb when he's a mug like you, a man who could get the confidence of bankers and sell them smart ideas, as you did. You could have dropped your crooked ways and made a good living at that game."

Belmann snorted. "And you're smart, huh?"

"Smarter than you," Satan said mildly, and sat back in the cushions.

He closed his eyes and listened to the purr of the wheels as they broke into the open and started across the Jersey Meadows. The air was balmy, and from high above came the drone of an airplane motor.

CHAPTER 15
THE LAST MILE

SATAN SAT straight when the automobile made a turn along a deserted road and nosed for a small factory that bore a sign reading, NEW-LITH STONE COMPANY. But he didn't appear overly interested, sinking back a moment later.

"How'd you make that fifty thousand dollars you had tucked away, Belmann? Who'd you steal that from."

"Steal, nothing!" the man said hotly. "Commissions on vault sales, commissions on architects I hired, on stationery for all the banks, on furniture, lighting fixtures, alarm systems—"

Satan cut in, "And on phony time clocks, overcharging

Raphael and Krantz on guns, and on some other little honest deals, eh? I just wanted to know. I'm always curious about how a guy makes his money… whose it is. This is really yours, isn't it?"

"I sweated for that," Belmann growled. He grinned wickedly. "But, Satan—how you're going to sweat for cutting our racket short!" He cut off when the car slid to a stop, blew its horn twice, then started down the road again.

Satan appeared to be unconscious of the reason for the quick move. An automobile was coming down the street behind them. The driver raced on, turned suddenly in a sharp *U*, came back again. A plane droned high overhead, buzzing like a bee. The car came abreast the stone works again, slowed and turned in the driveway of the place. It nosed past huge trucks, twisted around some heavy rocks, came to a halt.

"The last mile has been clocked up, Satan," Belmann said. "Get out, and get out carefully."

Satan sat still. "Ladies first," he said.

Pam Pollarde was too frightened to move. The driver stood looking in a moment, then yanked the door open. "Say! Did you see that car that came along when I was stopping the first time? Don't many cars come this way! No, sir. Wonder who them guys were?" He seemed nervous.

"Let's wonder about unloading," Belmann snapped. "Yank that door open and step this dame down. What's the delay?"

Pam was jerked roughly out of her seat by the burly chauffeur. Belmann prodded Satan. "Come on, Satan. Get going, or I'll let you have it right here!"

Satan was climbing to his feet when two men came hurrying around the corner of the rock and over to the car. One of them, tall, with a small, cruel mouth above which a hawk nose hovered, glowered at Belmann with nasty eyes. Satan looked at the youngish face of him, and the white hair—and wondered.

"How could such a young man be so old looking?" he wondered. But his question was answered with Belmann's words.

"Rafe, I hurried all I could. I had to stop at the office, on my way. Last minute tracks to cover up."

"But I told you to come as soon as I got word that Krantz had been bumped and the dough tagged!"

Belmann leaned forward, jerking his thumb at Satan. "Besides, Rafe—look who I brought for company! Do you recognize him?"

Raphael Gartano, master counterfeiter, blinked and looked at Satan. Then, suddenly, Belmann reached out and pulled Satan's cap from his head.

"Satan!" Gartano gasped, his eyes going wide. He stared at Belmann in astonishment. "You—got Satan? *You?*"

Belmann glowered. "He's not so tough! I took him like a kid picking up marbles."

Gartano stared suspiciously at Satan for a moment, then shrugged. He looked at Pam. "Who is the dame?"

"My secretary," Belmann answered. "She knows too much. Wasn't safe to leave her there."

Arnleigh said, "I'll see that she doesn't speak, Rafe."

"Aw, you mugs," the counterfeiter grunted. "You and your having to stop at offices, and Arnleigh with having to drag dames along." He shook his head, eyed Satan suspiciously again, as if he sensed trouble.

"Look at the plane," the driver said, and gaped up into the air.

Gartano stood watching Satan, his eyes hardening. "You killed my pal, Krantz?"

Satan grinned. "Seems to me I did," he said. "Krantz and *his* little pals. I also killed another member of the Krantz gang, after you decided it was safer to jump that cotton out of Saugerville than leave it there when I was in the field against you. Likewise, I tied up three of your finger men who were working at Tayloe City. Now, if I can only get you, Raphael, I'll die happy... some day."

Gartano's face went black with rage. "Get down, you rat! I'll take you in back, in my workshop, and kill you by inches! I'll roll stones weighing two tons over your frame, an inch at a time. You'll see your own guts and blood being squeezed out of you! Your eyes will pop from your head like grapes!"

THE MAN slid a gun from his pocket and stood back. Satan climbed down and walked stiff-legged a few feet, then turned. The chauffeur was still gaping into the air. Arnleigh and Belmann got out of the car.

"Hey! Look at that plane! Look how close down it is. Cripes, is it goin' to land in the road?"

There was a sharp whistling sound in the air. Gartano and the others looked, startled, their eyes going up momentarily. Satan moved swiftly but purposefully. He slammed against Pam Pollarde, knocking her into the body of the car through the open door. Then he kicked the door shut and jerked his arms down, hard, in the same motion.

Twin .45s skinned down and into sight from under the wide sleeves of his polo coat, where they had hung suspended near the elbows on rubber-bands. Gartano cursed and tried to get his gun into play. But Satan's first two slugs caught him in the neck, slammed him to the ground.

Belmann screamed hysterically and clawed to get his hand out of his pocket... and his gun with it. But Satan blasted him back against the car, dropped him with a bullet through the brain. The chauffeur was running madly for the rear of the stone works. Satan fired with his left hand, brought the man down with a brace of bullets in his left leg.

And then Arnleigh came into the picture.

He had a .38 in his hand, was crouched behind the car and firing at Satan. The crew leader jumped for the front of the car, craftily climbed up on the front bumper as a rain of lead tore under the ground and ravaged the dirt where Satan's feet would have been.

The plane was lower, now, was settling for a landing in the road. Shouts were coming from the rear of the stone works. Satan held his fire when Arnleigh presented an inviting target through the rear window of the car. Pam Pollarde might rise up at any moment, he knew, frenzied by the uproar of the battle.

A car horned repeatedly as it roared down the road, sliding to a stop near the airplane whose wheels were slowing. Men poured out of that cockpit... masked men... with tommy-guns and automatics ready. They swarmed up on the running board of the automobile, clung to it desperately as the car swung and bounced up the rutted drive for the stone works.

A crew of gunners burst into view from the back of the plant; but they were met by the hellish fire that poured at them from that automobile. They took a few pot shots, turned when the raking bursts of lead became unbearable, dashed for cover.

Satan's crew jumped down from the running boards and went after them. Others, who weren't in time to get aboard the car, were running up the drive, the racket of their guns raising a hideous uproar. Arnleigh skittered around from the back of the car, his .38 raised to pick off a crew man. Satan put his foot up on the radiator of the car and dived, knocking the man flat. His gun exploded harmlessly in the dirt.

Satan was on his feet like a cat, the blood flowing from a gash in his cheek. He dragged Arnleigh to his feet, smashed him in the mouth with a hard right, then slammed him into the car with a steam-hook. The big gunman sobbed brokenly. Slim ranged alongside, his eyes hard.

"You hurt, Captain?"

Satan shook his head. "Handcuffs, Slim." He knocked the .38 out of Arnleigh's hand and snapped the wristlets on him. The firing from the rear of the place ceased abruptly.

Satan's men came into view, herding a sorry-looking gang in front of them. Slim yanked a spare mask from his pocket and passed it to Satan. The leader donned it, walked past his men and to where Raphael Gartano lay, gasping his life out. Two ragged tears in his neck showed that he was beyond saving... for the Hot Seat. The man's eyes opened as the crew leader ranged alongside.

"That—fool—of a Belmann," he gasped. "How—did you do it?"

Satan walked to the car Belmann had brought him in, reached up to the roof of it, pried something loose from the top. He came back, held it so that the sun flashed from its glittering surface.

"Before I let Belmann '*capture*' me," Satan said, "I stuck this mirror on the roof of his car. My men, in a plane flying above the city, merely followed the flashes of the thing and had the car covered every foot of the way out. Another car followed Belmann's merely by watching where the plane was going. Simple, eh? I could have taken Belmann any time. But what I wanted was you. I let him lead me to you."

Gartano's lips twisted in a wry grimace. "You got me—you devil—but you'll never get my money!"

Satan smiled. "Don't let that bother you, Raphael. We've already found it."

The man's eyes widened. "You—found that—big rock with the white face, and—cracked it?"

Satan swung slightly. "Slim! Look for a rock with a white face and crack it."

Gartano's eyes were full of hatred. "You stinking rat! You—you copper!"

"Thanks," Satan said. "That's a compliment, Gartano. Anything I can do for you before you die? You're going, you know!"

Gartano nodded slightly. His eyes were filming. "How—did you guess about Belmann?" he gasped.

Satan shrugged. "He was the only man who could have gotten the bankers' fingerprints, tricked up their time locks, sold them on new buildings, purchased the phony stone for the banks. And one very important thing—he was the only one who could have kidded me into thinking I was being followed from Brayton, when it was really Belmann himself who had me tracked by two thugs. It all added up, Raphael. But if there was one clincher in the thing, it was the fact that I checked the Treasury Department and found he had *not* reported phony money!"

Raphael Gartano died a moment later... went to meet a Judgement whose eternal coin he could not hope to counterfeit.

CHAPTER 16
RAINBOW'S END

S LIM AND the crew were gathered in silence as Satan went rapidly over the stacks of money that had been brought from hiding in the false-front rock.

Satan said, "Well... estimating that the Bank of Brayton lost one hundred and fifty thousand, instead of seventy-five—and that the losses of the other two banks total three hundred thousand—which we'll have to return—that doesn't leave so much."

The Chink stirred. "Maybe there's five dollars apiece left?"

Satan chuckled. "After I take down my one-third... from which I pay all expenses... you boys split the rest in even lots.

That gives you—" he calculated rapidly, "about seven thousand dollars apiece for these few days' work."

Solly fainted.

When he came to, Pam Pollarde was sitting near Satan, taking down his words in shorthand.

"…That's the report for the Treasury Department, and the F.B.I.," he said. He smiled slightly. "And don't mistake another mug for a Treasury man, Miss Pollarde—as you did last time! Remember—when one of Bellman's stooges came and said the bills were Raphael's?"

The girl flushed. Solly looked interested.

"Now," Satan went on. "You have your reports made out. Next, you warn all the *new* banks, in person, over the telephone. Then… you will return the money we have recovered to the banks that rightfully claim it."

The girl's eyes grew round. "You're trusting me with such an amount of money?"

"Not quite," Satan said, with a slight cough. "One of my men will go with you. I haven't decided which one, yet. But you must swear that you won't reveal him as one of my crew."

"So help me," Pam Pollarde said.

Solly's head was cocked on one side. He came close, said something in his native tongue. The girl crimsoned and jumped to her feet, slapping him soundly. The crew roared. Satan stared.

"Solly? What was that you said to Miss Pollarde?"

The eagle-beaked member gestured with both hands spreading wide. "Miss *Pollarde?* Huh! Miss Politzsky, maybe you mean. I said to her, in Yiddish, 'You're pretty and I'd like to kiss you.'"

The meeting threatened to break up in gales of laughter. Satan snapped the men's minds back to business.

"This mob is stretched out, cuffed and waiting for the Sams," he said. "We split here. Kayo takes the plane. Slim and I take the car. The rest of you will unmask and hike out of here at intervals. I'm advancing you more expense money to hire automobiles to take you home. I'm not going to see you lads again... until the next time. Slim will meet with you tomorrow night to close up headquarters, pay you off, and attend to any details."

CARY ADAIR paced the priceless rug of his living room impatiently. Jeremy had just announced Adair's old friend, Joe Desher, of the F.B.I.

The outside buzzer rang and Jeremy walked into the foyer hall.

"Come in, Mr. Desher," he said.

Jo Desher bustled into the luxurious room and crossed to Adair, shaking his hand warmly. "Well, Cary, how's the old loafer?" He paused, leaned close. "How did you burn your face?"

"I was lighting a cigarette, and the box of matches caught fire. Damn careless of me," Adair said drily. "How are tricks, Jo?"

The F.B.I. man shook his head. "Slow."

"Slow? But, that business up at—was it *Brayton?* What happened to that, Joe?"

Desher rocked on his heels for a moment. "Closed business," he said. "In some way, my old friend Satan got in on it and ran it to the ground. Krantz and Raphael Gartano, the cracksman and the counterfeit king, are gone... dead—thanks to Satan."

He scratched his chin. "Damn it all, Cary—this is one of the times I'd like to take that chap by the hand and say, 'Thank you!'"

"Do it by proxy," Adair suggested, a glint in his eye. "Shake my hand and say it… and we'll drink on it! Maybe Satan will somehow know that you feel that way!" He turned. "Jeremy!"

The gaunt, melancholy manservant slid into the room instantly, a tray on his hand and two drinks on the tray. "Yes, sir."

Desher clutched the drink in one hand and Adair's strong, browned hand in the other. "Satan, old friend—wherever you are—Thank you!"

"Cheerio," Adair murmured grimly.